MW01228625

This Book is dedicated to my Mother Dorothy Elizabeth Hartman. She has always been there for me with all her love and care.

All the characters in this book are fictitious, and any resemblance to actual persons living or dead is purely coincidental.

Revised Edition, October 17 2017

Special thanks to Janet Stout and Dorothy Menasco

By 1880 the big cattle drives were over. The open land was closed by cattlemen, farmers and settlers. Fences were put up and all the big cattle trails were no longer useable. With the railroads coming closer to a lot of towns most drives were three hundred miles or less. To attempt a cattle drive that the Lassiter Ranch was preparing to do was all but impossible.

The Last Drive

Early May, Pigeon Forge Tennessee 1893. A sunny morning with a light breeze.
It was a cool and crisp with birds chirping and horses snorting as Brad was feeding the chickens and picking up eggs. He waved at Max Basford and Rick Peters as they were taking care of feeding the livestock and getting ready for the men from the mill to come for the teams they needed to move the lumber for local shipment and to the rail depot for loading on flat cars. He stopped for a moment to glance at the grave of his wife and son. Then he went to the house.

  Brad went inside and Patti was making breakfast, it smelled so good with the aroma of bacon filling the kitchen.

 "Good morning Patti, sleep well?" He asked. "Sure smells good in here."

"Yes Brad, I slept very well thank you. And you?"

"Yes I did Patti. There's a little chill in the air this morning and it won't be very much longer before the warmer weather will be on us."

Chapter One

Brad Lassiter was born on a cattle ranch near Lufkin Texas and nearby Nacogdoches, July 23rd 1861. He grew up there with his brother Steve who was born on the same day as Brad one year later. He excelled in learning the cattle trade and started at an early age with his brother going on cattle drives with his Dad, Charles Lassiter. By the age of fifteen he was a first class drover helping to drive cattle to the stock yards for sale. He learned the way of the land and the animals that lived there. He also learned the way of the Indians that shared this vast open land. He was handy with a gun and very good shot. At the age of twenty five with the cattle business in decline and fewer drives to market he decided to join the U.S. Cavalry and served two years fighting rogue Indian bands and cattle rustlers. It was at Fort Scott he met Judy Owen and after dating for a time they married. They had a very nice wedding at the Lassiter ranch and her father came all the way from Pigeon Forge, Tennessee to be there. They moved into the Lassiter home planning to build a house of their own on the ranch property. Judy was a big help to Brads Mom, Becky, who loved having her around and helping her to bake, cook and caring for the house and yard.

They were married almost six months when Judy told Brad she was pregnant. Everyone was excited with the prospects of a young'en around the ranch again. And Miss Becky couldn't wait to spoil the child. They carried on the chores at the ranch for several months, and Brad was working on building their home about a hundred yards from the main house when a rider came riding up.

Charlie Lassiter went to meet him. "Can I help ya?" he asked.

"Lookin' for Judy Lassiter, got a telegram for her" he replied.

Charlie went to house and got Judy. She went to the rider and thanked him for his service. She opened the folded paper and in a few minutes she fell to her knees weeping.

"Oh my God she cried, oh dear lord."

Brad ran up to her and asked, "What's the matter Judy?" She handed him the telegram. It read;

You need to come home, stop.

Your father has passed on to the Lord, stop.

Regretfully and sorrowfully, Max, stop

(Telegrams said stop at the end of each sentence because you couldn't put a period as that would have been a letter.)

After consoling Judy the best I could, I suggested we eat and get to bed early so we can pack a wagon and get an early start to the train depot for the long ride to Pigeon Forge, Tennessee.

The next morning Judy and I climbed on the buckboard and my brother Steve rode with us to bring the wagon back. It was a long train ride, changing trains three times to make the connection to Knoxville as that was the closest we could get to Pigeon Forge by train. Judy had telegrammed Mr. Peters to meet us there and when we arrived he was waiting for us with a buckboard and a saddled horse. Mr. Peters gave his regrets to Judy, and she asked how he died. Mr. Peters said Doctor Schaeffer said it was consumption, (which in those days was a term for a heart attack) Judy got on the wagon with Mr. Peters and I mounted the horse and we road on to her father's home that sat along the Little Pigeon River just outside of town. The first thing she asked was to see her father's grave site. It was in a grassy lot about a hundred feet behind the house. It still had the flowers left by well wishers who attended the funeral. She kneeled down and started to cry as she softly spoke to him. What she said I do not know and I thought it was none of my business. Oh sure, I felt so bad for her, losing her Dad so soon, but I felt what she said to him was between them. When she stood up I took her hand and we walked to the house to put our things in order.

Her father had a mercantile shop selling clothes and whole goods, hardware, tools, and he also had a livery stable that rented out horse teams, mostly used by the men working for the lumber mill. Her father had left a will and all was in order and we started about the task of taking over where he left off. Mr. Rick Peters and Mr. Max Basford agreed to stay on running the stable and Mrs. Patti Fogt was staying on to run the mercantile shop. A couple of months went by quickly and all was running smoothly. I had to go over the mountain to meet Noah Ogle, who had a store in Gatlinburg to pick up a shipment for our store that was dropped off there by mistake. I told Judy to be careful as she was due at anytime and that I would be back the next day. I left early in the morning and was going to stay over night in Gatlinburg. I got there that afternoon and met Mr. Ogle and he showed me the boxes of goods that I was to get. All was in order and I shook his hand and thanked him. I checked into the Inn near by and had a good meal and would load up and leave early the next morning.

That night I was sound asleep but the noise of a rider coming hard down the street woke me up. After all the years on the cattle trails and being in the service with the cavalry made me a light sleeper and attuned to the threat of danger. There was a commotion down stairs and I heard a man calling my name in an anxious voice. Next I heard someone running up the stairs. I grabbed my pistol just to make sure I was ready for what ever it could be in case someone meant me harm. There was a banging on my door and Mr. Rick Peters called my name. I ran to the door to meet him.

"What's the matter?" I asked as I opened the door.
"You must come quickly." He nervously answered.

"Why?' I quizzed. "It's Miss Judy," Rick answered, "there has been an accident."

"What kind of accident?'

"She tripped and fell down the stairs. We got Doc Schaffer to come over and he said to get you immediately." He replied.

My God I thought, what next, is she going to be OK? I thought to myself as I grabbed my belongings and we ran down the stairs to the horses. I didn't give a damn about the whole goods they could wait... We rode hard over the mountain and got to the house in what seemed like days although it was two to three hours, I don't really know. When we rode up Doctor Fred Schaffer came out to meet us.

"Sorry Mr. Lassiter, I did all I could."

I looked at him and asked, "What do you mean all you could?" I quizzed?

"She's gone my friend, and the baby also! I am so sorry young man!"

My God I thought, as I ran into the house this can't be happening. She's to young and the baby too! I went to her side and held her lifeless body for I do not know how long. Mr. Peters, Mr. Basford and Miss Patti and her husband stood by and no one spoke for a long time. The Undertaker, Mr. Donald Moore, who was also the local preacher, came in and made it official, and gave his respects. "I won't take her until your ready Mr. Lassiter." He said with his head lowered.

I looked at him, "Give me a couple more minutes" I replied. He shook his head and stepped out of the room with the others. I could not believe this was happening. My Son was lying next to her wrapped in a blanket. He looked as he was sleeping peacefully, never to know what his role in life could have been. I gave Mr. Moore the nod and he and the others helped him take their lifeless bodies out. I sat and cried for I don't know how long. Miss Patti had made some coffee and brought me a cup. I sat and sipped on my cup slowly until it was gone.

"Want some more coffee?" She asked.

"Miss Patti I think I will just go to bed." She nodded her head and said she would be by in the morning. I went to our room and it was suddenly so empty. Soon it was day light and I was lying on my back with my eyes open. This had to be a bad dream, I thought. Suddenly, all in my life was gone. And the son I never got to show the ways of life too! Never to watch him grow and share his life with us. All is gone, just gone!

The funeral was heart wrenching. We buried my son with her, it seemed fitting to do so. We had a little gathering at the house afterwards. Patti had prepared some food and cookies for the people, a lot of whom I didn't know. They offered their condolences' and sorrow.

For the next couple of days I moped around, feeling lost and abandoned. What do I do now? What should I do? Mr. Basford and Mr. Peters said that they would continue on as long as I needed them. Miss Patti asked if I would keep the store open. I told her as long as she could help run it while I made up my mind as to what I should do. What must I do? After days of thinking it over, my mind kept telling me that Judy would want me to keep things going and carry on my life. I missed her so much. She really was my first true love. Somehow I felt at times she was in whatever room I was in, just looking over my shoulder. At times I swear I saw someone or something move out of the corner of my eye. Time passed slowly, it was such a lonely feeling. I worked with Mr. Peters and Mr. Basford to learn the livery trade and went with Mrs. Fogt to the store quite a few times to catch up on the retail business and meet customers. Patti really knew her job and did it well. She kept up the inventory and made up the orders for new goods and replacement items. The customers really liked her, and she had a knack about her that seemed to make the customers spend more freely than they would have if someone with less knowledge of the trade was handling the transactions. Several months went by and things seemed to be moving along very nicely. It was a learning experience, but I was catching on to it well.

Just about the time I thought all was going smoothly another calamity struck! Mrs. Fogt's husband didn't come home after a hunting trip in the mountains. Fearing he got lost or maybe injured, a search party was formed to go out and look for him

After a couple of days searching they found what was left of his body and they brought the remains back to Pigeon Forge. As far as could be figured he was killed by a bear or mountain lion. No one was really sure.

There was a funeral; a small gathering of well wishers and the Pastor, Mr. Moore, gave a nice sermon. After the service Mrs. Fogt came to me and said she was afraid she would have to quit as she now had no where to stay. I asked her why? She told me that she and her husband came from Ohio to move eventually west, looking for a new place to find work. They stopped at Pigeon Forge and he decided to go to work at the lumber mill. The reason she had no place to stay was that Mr. Fogt had made arrangements with the mill owners to stay in a shed on the mill property. I had no idea she was living like that!

After talking with Patti about her plight I asked if she would move in the house with me as I had several rooms I was not using. At first she seemed nervous but I explained to her it was strictly a professional arrangement and I would consider it part or her payment for her job. She agreed and moved in with what few belongings she had and settled into the west room up stairs. It worked out well. She kept the home tidy and even made the meals, which was just fine with me. Finally I had all in order and running so smooth. What else could possibly go wrong?

I put the eggs on the counter and sat at the table. Patti poured me a cup of coffee.

"Your breakfast will be ready in just a few moments," She said.

"Sure smells good," I replied, "got a big day planned Miss Fogt?'

"Just the usual, mostly. I got to finish hemming a dress I sold to Mrs. Moore, the preacher's wife and I am going to make up some more men's neckties from some of the left over material we have in our stock."

She served breakfast and sat down and ate her breakfast. "Gotta' get going," she said, "I don't want to open late. We have been quite busy. Seems like, we are getting more new people moving into and around town every day."

"Yes it seems that way," I said. "I hope you have a pleasant day and I will see you this evening. I am going to the mill and meet with the owners and collect this month's horse rental and check to see if they have any needs. Then Max and I are going to look at some horses a man has for sale. I'll clean up so you can go."

She thanked me and got herself ready to leave for work.

I met with the mill owners and all seemed well with them, then I got with Max and we went to look at the horses for sale. We bought a couple nice draft horses and took them to the blacksmith to have shoes put on them. All was going real well now, finally…

CHAPTER TWO

A few days went by with no more excitement. That was a relief! I was talking with Rick, as we were now pretty much on a first name basis, and a rider came up.

"Mr. Rudolph has a telley for you," he said, "I would have brought it to you but he said he wanted to see you anyway."

"Thank you," I answered, "I'll go pick it up" A telegram I thought? Who was it from? Hope all is well at the ranch; hope Mom and Dad are OK. I saddled up and rode down to the post office where Bob Rudolph worked and ran the telegraph ticker. He loved anything to do with electronics. I rode up and tethered my horse and went in.

"How's it going, Mr. Rudolph?"

"Just fine young man," he answered, "Got a telegram for ya, but first I want to tell you the big news. We are getting a telephone set up here in a month or so. Then we can talk over the wire. That will really be something. You need to sign up for one. There is no telling what comes next the way things are going with electric gadgets. And you know what young man?" he quizzed, "Some day we will be sending pictures over the wire and carry a telephone with us somehow. Not sure how, but I want to bet ya, I can see that happening"

"The telephone sounds great. Who are you going to call?" I asked.

"Anyone that will listen," he replied laughing, "If they or you got one. Here's your telley."

It was folded, I opened it, and it read.

Need you at the ranch as quick as you can stop
Have some very important business to handle stop
Let me know how soon you can get here stop
I don't have time to fool around stop
   Dad

I was puzzled. What could be going on? I thought to myself.

"Mr. Rudolph, can you send a reply?' I asked

"Sure can young man. Write it out and I'll send it right away. That will cost ya two bits." (Two bits, is twenty five cents.)

I wrote back;

Dad what is so important? Is all OK with you and Mom? I got a lot of things going on here taking over the business I inherited, and it's a full time job.
Brad.

I gave it to Bob and paid him. "I'll send it right away, and if a reply comes in I'll let you know ASAP." Bob said.

"Thank you just let me know." I answered, went out and got on my horse and left. I couldn't think of what could be going on. He had a good bunch of men working for him. They could handle any business he had going on. Couldn't they handle it? I was thinking. Riding by the shop I figured

I would stop and see how Miss Patti was doing. When I entered the store she was busy making some men's neckties. "How's it going Patti?" I asked.

"Been busy," she answered, "quite a few customers this morning. Got Mrs. Moore's dress finished, and she was very pleased. How's your day so far?"

"Well I got a telegram from my Dad. He's got something going on and wants me to come back to the ranch to help." I told her.

"I hope all is OK." She answered. "You don't need any more excitement for a while that's for sure."

"You're right about that." I said. "I'm finally getting to know what I am doing and keeping up with it. I'm going to the stable, see you tonight Miss Patti."

"Have a good afternoon Brad."

I rode to the stable to see how Max and Rick were doing. They had all the stalls cleaned and the barn floor cleared. Max handed me the money he collected from the men that rented the teams for the day and from some who rented for several days.

"We don't have a draft horse or a mule left for rent." He said "Been busy today, only have a couple of riding horses left to rent"

"That's good, Max. We may have to buy some more if the mill keeps going like it is. I'll run down to the bank and put this money in, I'll see you later." I got on my horse and went back into town. All the time my mind was thinking about what could be going on at the ranch? I just can't leave everyone and go. Oh sure I thought, Max, Rick, and Miss Patti could handle it, they were really good at what they do, and been doing it for years, but I hate to put more pressure on them. There has been enough trauma, I thought to myself. I rode to the bank to deposit the money. When I dismounted Mr. Love was walking by, he was one of the men that owned and ran the lumber mill.

"Hello Mr. Love," I said. "Things been busy for you?"

"Yes Mr. Lassiter, very busy," he replied, "Got a lot of timber being cut, and if it wasn't for your horses we could not keep up with the distribution of it."

"Glad to be of help, I might have to get more horses," I said to him.

"We are keeping up with it so far, but if it keeps up like this you may need some more," he said, "gotta' get back to work Mr. Lassiter, you have a good day."

I thanked him and bid him good day, and went into the bank to make the deposit. On returning to my horse Mr. Rudolph hollered over to me. "Gotcha a reply, he said. I walked over to him and took the telegram, it said:

I don't have time to fool around son stop
Get your tail over here quickly we are burning money stop
I will pay for you train ticket stop

Leave tomorrow stop
I will have Steve pick you up stop
I am sitting here waiting for your answer stop
Good heavens, I thought, Dad just doesn't get it. He wants me to race over there like it's just over the hill and I don't have anything else to do! I went back into the Post office and wrote a reply. I told him this better be very serious and I would leave on the first train I could get the next morning. I paid Bob to send it and rode back to the house to pack, and I was not excited about it. I told Max what was going on and told him I would send him a telegram when I found out what was happening and how long before I would get back. He said they could handle it and not to worry. When Miss Patti came home I told her of the goings on and hoped she would be alright with running things. I knew she could, but I wanted to let her know I just didn't want to leave her over burdened. She said it would not be a problem and Max and Rick would be there if she needed them.

"Not to worry, things will be fine." She told me. "Go get done what your Dad needs you to do and return home safely."

After dinner I sat and chatted with Mrs. Fogt a while before retiring to bed. I got up the next morning early and Max drove me to train depot and dropped me off. The train came early which was a surprise. I got on board and found myself a seat, there were plenty.

The train ride was long and tiring, but we made good time and the train transfers were on time. It was a little before noon the next day when the conductor cried "Lufkin, prepare to meet your doom, get your wits about you and keep your money in your pocket. And don't turn your back on anyone! Good luck." That wasn't very comforting. Had Lufkin changed that much in the short time I've been away? I tried to get what sleep I could on the train with all the noise and hustle, but I was still very tired. I think I was worn out more by the boredom. I just can't sit with out something to do. I got my belongings and got off the train. Steve waved at me and I walked to the buckboard to load up.

"How you doing Steve? Your lookin' good, put on a little weight I see." We gave each other a big bear hug. It was good to see him.

"Just a little," he answered, "Moms cooking will do that to you. How you doing? Looks like you can use some of her cooking too, long ride?"

"Yes, long and tiring, what is going on that's got Dad in such an uproar?"

"I'll let him tell you but I got to warn you, you ain't gonna like it." Steve replied.

"O K, let's get to the ranch brother, and let him tell me."

Lufkin has really gotten big, I didn't recognize it, There were plenty of saloons to entertain workers and cowboys in so many ways. The lumber business and the railroad has really put Lufkin on the map.

We got to the ranch and it looked like everyone was busy doing something. Buddy Perryman, one of Dads drovers for years came over to greet me.

"Howdy Brad, how are you doing my friend?" I hear you've had some tough time since I last saw ya. Sorry about your loss."

"Had some ups and downs but until this, things have smoothed out." I told him.

'Where's Dad?"

"He's out driving in some cattle from the thickets and the hills. We got quite a few to get branded and ready to move."

"Taken them to Abilene?" I asked

"Naw, I'll let your Dad fill you in, sounds exciting, and crazy, but exciting just the same. You know your Dad. When he gets an idea in his head the only one that can change his mind is your Mom most times, but not on this venture." Buddy told me.

Well it looks like some sort of cattle drive is planned, I figured, but why does he need me? He has plenty of good drovers, the best there is, and most of them have been working on the Lassiter ranch for years. The big cattle drives are over now days with railroads close to most ranches. I walked into the house and Mom came up and gave me a big hug.

"How are you doing son?" She asked. "Are you hungry? You look tired."

"I could use a bite to eat, if it's no trouble, haven't had a decent meal for a day or so and I am worn out from traveling." I told her.

"No problem son, I'll get you a bowl of stew and some bread. Want tea or coffee?" She asked.

"Coffee would be good Mom. So what's Dad in such a thither over?"

"I'll let him tell you Brad, when he gets in. He's been working from dawn to dusk, I don't agree, but his mind is made up and there's no changing it. You know how he can be."

The Lassiter's have had the ranch since 1800. My Dad Charles Lassiter, called Charlie by all was born in 1837 and took over the ranch after the war in 1866. My Grand Father, Charles Sr. was killed by bushwhackers. Most think it was by Confederate sympathizers in reprisal to bad feelings about his dealings with the Confederate Government over cattle purchases. When they stopped paying in silver or gold and offered Confederate money Charles senior refused to sell to them. This made the Confederates angry and they just started taking what they wanted by raids on the ranch and called him a Yankee supporter. The fact was he thought of Texas as his country, not the Confederacy. The Berman's who now have a small ranch near Nacogdoches, not far from the Lassiter's have been in and out of this area for years and were also thought of bushwhacking Old Charlie. They have been accused of stage robbery, cattle rustling and just about anything else that was illegal but no one could ever prove it or put Glen Berman or his son Rhett anywhere near whatever took place, and most people just looked the other way for their own good and safety!

I sat and ate the stew Mom got for me and drank my coffee; it was so tasty and filling. We sat and talked and I got her up to date with my new endeavors. Mom caught me up on the news since I left. She said Dad would be back just before dark. He was with Joe Parmer, AK and Arnie Arnold rounding up strays. At least he was in good company. Buddy Perryman and Joe Parmer have been close friends and worked for the ranch for years. Arnie has been the trail boss on drives for as long as I can remember. Dad brought A K to the ranch in 1876.

He was a Sioux Indian whose full name was Akecheta Otaktay, which in Sioux language meant, Warrior Kills Men. Because his name was hard to pronounce we nicknamed him A K. He was a wiry built man with a chiseled face and cold dark eyes, tight lipped, cold hearted and like a cat on the prowl. Never said much unless he had to. He fought in the Custer Battle at the Little Bighorn before joining the Lassiter ranch, but never said which side he was on and no one had the courage to ask. Dad found him badly wounded when he passed through the Little Bighorn battlefield returning from a cattle drive in the Wyoming Territory. Dad and his men nursed him back to health. He would have died for sure, if they hadn't found him. A K said he would work for Dad as long as he was able and swore allegiance to the Lassiter Ranch for saving him. A K was a good man to have on a drive. He knew and understood the land and Nature. He could smell trouble and was very handy with a gun or a knife.

Chapter Three

 Mom went on into the kitchen to start the meal for tonight
and I took my coffee and went out and sat on the swing
bench on the porch. There was a nice breeze coming out
from the north and it felt good. I sat thinking of all sorts of
things; my mind was running in circles. I watched men
branding cattle, moving cattle and horses. Things were very
busy, something was up all right but I just couldn't figure
out what it was. I got up and went out to see some of the
men I haven't seen since I left and there were men I did not
know. I talked to Mike Latimer, Lee Tingy, James Harrell,
Don Volsch, all have worked for Dad quite a while, and all
good drovers too. A drover helps herd the cattle on a drive.
Afterwards I went over to the shed where Steve Lowery,
the blacksmith was making horse shoes on the forge.
"Hi, Steve, how's it going? Got a lot of work to do?"
"Good to see you Brad. Yah I got to make some extra
shoes, sure to lose some where were going. Gonna be a
tough one that's for sure." He replied.
"And just where are we going Steve?"
"Oh it's gonna be something, that's for sure, but your Dad
told us all to keep our mouths shut and let him tell you
himself."

"Why all the secrecy Steve?" That's what everyone is telling me. Hope we are not up to no good, or breaking the law."

"Nah, nothing like that Brad, it's up and up but it's got complications though. Your Dad's got it in his head and ain't nobody gonna change his mind. But as long as we are getting paid, we'll ride."

"Well Steve, been good talking with you."

"You too, Brad, see you later."

I walked over to the coral and saw Carlon James, he was the newest man on the ranch took over as wrangler about a year before I left the ranch. A wrangler is in charge of the horses on a drive. He was talking to Matt Yeaton and Howard Branden both drovers for Dad for a few years, and good men.

"Howdy Carlon, keeping those nags in good shape." I asked.

"Nags, what ya mean nags? Your Dad has collected some fine horses here, no nags in this bunch." He said.

"That's good look-in buckskin you got there, Carlon, well built and stocky." I told him.

"Yah she's a pretty one that's for sure, your Dad said you always liked them buckskins. It's gonna be good to have you along again, it's always been good to be on a drive with you."

"Well I never said I was going on a drive, I don't even know what's happening or where it's going. Besides that, I got so much going on back in Tennessee." Matt and Howard had an evil grin on their faces.

"Your ole man will fill you in, that's for sure, Brad." Matt said with a smile on his face. Then I heard the clanging of the time to eat bell at the bunk house.

"Gotta wash up and get some fixins' Brad, talk to ya later" Matt said.

I shook hands with the three of them and went back to the house. Before I got there riders were coming in with a bunch of cattle and moved them into the coral. It was Dad, AK, Arnie and Joe Parmer and a couple of Vaqueros pushing them in. They looked worn out. Dad looked over and saw me, he got off his horse and quickly walked to me.

"So good to see you son, glad you made it OK." He said and gave me a crunching hug. He was a stocky strong man.

"Doing good Dad, looks like you got some sun today."

"Today? I've been getting sun for days boy, gotta' lot to do in the next couple of days, I'll tell you over dinner. Gotta' get washed up first, your Mom wouldn't feed me unless I did and besides I gotta' get this salt off me from sweating. Meet ya in the house." He patted me on the back and went to the wash shed. As I walked to the house my mind was thinking. If he's got all these men, very capable men at that, I'll listen to his pitch and politely turn him down to get back to Tennessee and resume my new ambitions. I know he's going to fuss, but that's Dad and he'll get over it in time. I washed up a little and went to the dinning room where Mom was getting a nice meal laid out.

"Want a drink Brad," she asked, "Your Dad is going to have one. He always does before dinner you know."

"Yes Mom I think I will, probably going to need one. From what I've been seeing and what little I've heard. Dads got some behemoth plan to pitch to me." I said with a smile. Mom poured me a nice glass full.

"Made at a still run by old John Boger up in the hills. You remember John don't you?"

"Yes Mom, I do, he is a tough ole bird."

John Boger is the man who runs a chuck wagon on many of Dads drives. He really knew his job. Made meals out of nothing some times and other times, I probably didn't want to know what it was made of.

"As the drives got fewer he moved up in the mountains, built a cabin and shares it with an Indian woman." Mom told me.

"So Ole John's making whisky now." I replied. "Tastes real good too!"

"Yes he's been doing it for a while now," Mom answered, "He sells to a lot of the saloons in and around here. Some woman named Jean Osterhoudt has bought up a lot of

27

saloons in Lufkin and Nacogdoches and I hear say some other towns also. She buys liquor from John and I hear tell she is running other business ventures at the saloons from what they say. I won't go into any details but I think you get the gist of what I'm talking about." She said with a blush on her face.

"I think I get the meaning, Mom. I understand it's gotten a little rough in Lufkin, even the conductor warned us before we got off the train."

"Yes things have changed, Son, and not for the better. I try not to go into Lufkin anymore than I have too, and I don't go alone"

About that time Dad and my brother Steve came into the room. "I see you got a drink already son, let me get one and I'll join ya." He poured a good stiff one, Mom got a glass of wine and Steve got a beer from the kitchen. Dad sat at the head of the table, Mom brought out the rest of the meal, sat next to him.

"Sit gentlemen," he said. "Mom did a nice pork roast and mashed tatters and gravy."

"I've been smelling that meal cooking for a while Dad, I'm sure it's the best as always."

"Can't beat your Moms cooking," Dad proudly spoke and patted her on the shoulder.

Dad said grace and told us to dig in and we did. It was really very good, a super tender roast and all the fixins. We chatted back and forth sharing tales of present and past. Then finally, Dad spoke up!

"Well Son I guess you're ready to hear what I got going. And it's really gonna be something," he said with a serious look on his face. "We are getting ready to put on a cattle drive that hasn't been seen in years, a big one! I have amassed a herd of thirty five hundred head of cattle and we are going to drive them to St. Louis Missouri. We got to have them there before the end of August."

I was in shock, "St. Louis? Good lord Dad, have you lost your mind?" Steve tried to hide his smile. "Wichita or Abilene is only three hundred miles from here and you don't need me tagging along for that. Steve….., can't you talk him out of this?" Mom could see I was getting warm under the collar and started clearing off the table. As far as I was concerned this was madness.

"I'll let you gentlemen talk business." She said and started taking left overs to the kitchen. Steve was looking at the ceiling and I could see the glare in Dads eyes. He was not happy and he was not hiding it. "Son," he said angrily, "I am talking about more money then we have ever seen, One hundred forty seven thousand dollars. That's forty two dollars a head. Around here in Abilene we get twenty five to thirty dollars. A man named Swift, bought the old stock yard in East St. Louis and is building a packing house to haul beef to the east. We are one of four ranches he contacted. I don't know if the others are going to do it but, we are Son, and we will succeed."

"Dad, don't you realize most of the open range is closed to cattle drives, or has been bought up by land investors, ranchers and settlers? Kansas is closed to Texas cattle because of the tick fever our long horns carry. There are barbed wire fences all over, not to mention the mountainous regions we will have to travel. And besides that Dad, there are rustlers and rogue Indians all over between here and St. Louis. It's not the good old days we once knew." I said to him.

"My boy I know it's a big task" he answered, "but, we have done our homework.

With enough drovers we can herd and protect the cattle. A K with some help from his Indian friends has ridden the trail we are going to take. We will by-pass a lot of the problems and mountains by using old secret Indian trails that cut through the canyons. And most of the towns we can skirt around."

"You say most of the towns, Dad. But what about the ones we can't? There's a mighty big chance for serious problems, unforeseen dangers and that could spell disaster and loss of part or the entire herd!" I blurted back.

"We know it's not going to be a joy ride, Son but it's going to put almost thirty seven thousand dollars in you pocket, and that should be worth your trouble. I am giving fifty percent to split between you and Steve and Mom and I are taken the other fifty and pay the men out of that."

I just can't believe this whole plan. It sounds insane at the very least. Sure that's a lot of money but are we going to survive to use it, I was thinking. So many obstacles' not to mention the risks involved. We are going over some hard land that doesn't forgive, not in the least. And we will lose some steers, that's always the case but in this, well we could lose it all.

"Brad," Steve said, "I know what you're thinking but, "it can be done. We have planned this for quite a while and I am pretty sure we can pull it off."

"Pretty sure doesn't sound like a sound bet to me Steve. Not one I would gamble my life or savings on."

"Son" Dad interrupted, "We need you and we got to get out of here by this coming Monday. If I or the men we have didn't think we could do it we wouldn't try. They all know there is danger but they are confident we can get the job done."

"Dad it just sounds so risky. But it seems you and Steve are going to do it one way or an other and I can't let you two go it alone."

"Son" Dad answered, "We've got good men, and with you and your knowledge of the frontier it's not a push over, but doable. We will need a few more good men, and I have that plan ready to go, and I will need you to make that happen."

I sat there, my head was spinning. I couldn't let Dad down even as crazy as this plan was. With out me, he and Steve and the others are going to do it at all cost and means. And if I back out? Well Dad not only would be angry, but deeply hurt for a long time. I just couldn't let him and Steve take this risk all alone.

"OK Dad, what do you want me to do?"

Dad jumped up and gave me a hug that squeezed the breath out of me and Steve like to have broken my hand shaking it. They both thanked me several times!

Chapter Four

 I feel better now as there was no way I could let them go it alone. Oh sure there would be plenty of men with them but if something would happen and I wasn't there I could never forgive myself. This is going to be a tough drive and only Heaven and Mother Nature knows what will happen. Happen for sure, as this is not going to be easy. Dad has it set in his mind and no one, not even Mom, is going to change that. Dad said to wait a minute as he had something he wanted me to do tomorrow and left the room. He came back with some flyers in his hand.
"I want you to ride into Nacogdoches and Lufkin and post these anywhere that they can be seen." He said and handed them to me. "Need about four or five more drovers and with the money I'm paying I want good ones. I'll let you make the choices. Just make sure they are good hands. No slackers"
The flyers said;

Drovers wanted.
Paying $50 Dollars a month.
Three Meals a day
No Greenhorns
Meet Sunday morning at
Jeanne's Saloon 10 AM

In Lufkin, TX.
Be ready to ride.

That was very good money as most drovers made forty
dollars a month or less. And the average days pay today is
One Dollar and Eighty cents.

"Tomorrow is Thursday, so get them posted as soon as you
can Son, we need to roll out Monday morning."

"I'll get them out as soon as I get there." I replied.

"Good son, you will have them up by tomorrow afternoon
most likely. Stay in town till Sunday and be careful. Both
of those towns are rough and shady. And by the way, I
want you to pick up ten Winchester rifles in forty four forty
caliber, it will match our pistol ammo, or at least most of
them that is. And get five hundred rounds of bullets. I want
our men armed."

Dad handed me a wad of money and said. "That should
cover everything, my boy. I'm going to bed Son. Got a few
more cattle to herd up and check brands before
we move 'em out. We got the cattle in different staging
areas and joining 'em together as we drive north. Oh Son,
you need a horse! Did you see that pretty Buckskin Mare in
the wranglers corral?"

"Yes I did Dad she a beaut!"

"She's yours Son. I know how much you like Buckskins
and she sure is a top notch filly."

"Thanks Dad, I'll take good care of her."
"She'll take care of you to Son, she's a smarty! Well good night you two, we got a lot to do. See ya for coffee in the morning. Meet ya in bed Honey." He said to Mom. Dad shook my hand and Steve's and went upstairs. I checked with Mom to see if she needed any help and she said she was all done and ready to hit the bed after she washed up. I gave her a hug and went up to my room. How in Hades was I going to get any sleep? I have it seems, a million things to do. Gotta' telegram Miss Patti and let her know what's going on. I sure hope it doesn't put any strain on her or Max and Rick. I laid there and started thinking of some of the drives I did with my Dad for years. And most of them were good ones. Some had some challenges, Indians, rustlers, stampedes, and throw in a bear or a cougar once and a while, things could get testy. Wolves were not a big problem unless there were calves along, but Dad always brought along a few donkeys, and they would chase the wolves off. The thing I was most afraid of though was thunder storms. That could cause a stampede or you could get struck by lighting sitting high on that horse! John Boger, who we called Cookie, was always in charge of the chuck wagon. He was all the time griping and swearing at or about something. He did a great job of feeding us, and at times, entertained us with some good stories. One time when he was setting up our nooner', (after breakfast the

chuck wagon man rode ahead and found a suitable place for the cattle to graze, made coffee and eats for the men, then drove on to set up dinner). One time he was confronted by a couple of highway men who tried to rob him. Ole John distracted them enough so he could grab his pistol, killed one and wounded the other, who high tailed it out of there like a scared rabbit. John had himself a new pistol that he showed it off every time he had a chance. We also had another horse and saddle for the wrangler's herd.

I finally went to sleep and got up early morning. Mom had made coffee and gravy biscuits', Dad was already riding off with some men to round up more of the cattle. I went to the corral and saddled up my buckskin mare, she was sure nuff' pretty. A well built stocky horse. I named her Babe. I rode to Nacogodches first and I checked with some store owners and saloons and they let me put up our flyers. I told the barkeep in one of the saloons that I was going to Lufkin.

"Well you better watch yer' back," he told me, "That's one rough town now, not like it used to be. And you better check with the sheriff before you start hanging them signs up."

"Lufkin has really changed, hasn't it?" I replied.

"Sure has cowboy, they got a new sheriff. Names George Royal, came from down south somewhere, and he's trying to uphold the law there, but he's in fer a tough job. There's

so many ruffian's coming and going. And Jeanie's selling
more than liquor in her saloons, if ya know what I mean.
And no gun's allowed on ya' when you're in town. You'll
have to turn in your pistol to the sheriff when you get there.
But you better have a sneak gun or a knife to put on ya.
With all those saloons, ain't too many sober cowhands and
a fight can start any time for any reason. I try not to go
there unless I just gotta'.
"Thanks," I answered, "I'll keep my eyes and ears open.
Good day, and thanks for the warning."
"Good day cowman, be watchful and look over yer
shoulder, a lot." He told me.
 I rode on down to Lufkin and went to the sheriffs office.
Tied my horse to the rail and went on in. George Royal was
a well built fellow and a look in his eye that just seemed to
sparkle and a smile on his face. He appeared to be in his
mid thirties.
"Sheriff, can I ask you some questions?'
"Sure, don't know if I'll have the right answers." He said.
"I would like to put up some posters around town for hiring
some cow hands."
"Let me see what you have." I handed one to him and he
looked it over and said;
"You can put one on my bulletin board out front, but you
will have to ask the store and saloon owners before you

start hangin' 'em. And if you are staying, you'll need to turn in you pistol with me till you get ready to leave."

"That will be fine sir; I am staying till Sunday morning. They tell me you got a hard job ahead of you keeping the peace here."

"Always something going on here in town, God knows what's happening out side of town. I can't keep up with that, nor have the time too. Mostly drunken cowhands and fights over card games. If you have any trouble's arise come see me." George commented.

"Thank you sir," I answered and un-strapped my pistol belt and handed it to him. Before I left the ranch Dad gave me a derringer to keep in my pocket. I didn't hand that over. Just in case.

Chapter Five

I shook his hand and thanked him but before I could turn
to leave a deputy ran in the door.
"We got trouble brewing George! The Bermans just rode
into town." He exclaimed.
"Oh great, I better go out and meet em' and lay down the
rules. They can be trouble."
So far the Bermans hadn't caused Sheriff Royal any
serious problems, just drunk and disorderly and fighting in
the saloons wrecking furniture and fixtures, but Glen
Berman always paid the bill for the damage. George
adjusted his pistol belt and stepped outside.
"Mister Berman," he hollered, "Need to see ya."
"Howdy sheriff, just in town for a little relaxin', what can I
do for ya?"
"We got a new ordinance in town," the Sheriff said, "You
and your men will have to check your pistols if you are
staying Mr. Berman, if not you can ride on." He said with a
strong understanding in his tone of voice.
"Well sheriff, we ain't here to cause any fussin', nor do we
want any trouble," Glen Berman said, "We just want to
enjoy ourselves and take in the town's menu. Come on
boys, you heard the sheriff, turn 'em in like he said, we
don't wanta' break no laws"

The men and Berman went into the office and took off their
gun belts and turned them in. Sheriff Royal gave each man
a receipt for his belt and stacked them up on a shelf. He
thanked each man as he did. As they turned to leave Sheriff
Royal called out; "Mr. Berman, your reputation precedes
you sir. I need the gun in your boot I hear you carry also."
He demanded. Berman had a shocked look on his face
turned around and replied, "Golly sheriff, nearly done
forgot bout that. It's like part of my clothing, saved me
many times, but reckon I wont need it here will I.?" He
reached in his boot and pulled out a double barrel derringer
and handed it to the sheriff.
"Thanks, Mr. Berman; I certainly hope you won't need it."
George said with a grin on his face. Glen Berman's face
was red like a kid caught with his hand in the cookie jar.
"Hope you have a good time!" And he put the derringer on
the shelf with the other weapons.
"Well we will just have to see how it goes from here." he
said to me. "I hope your stay goes well and that you get the
men you need. By the way I didn't get your name."
"Brad, Brad Lassiter sir."   "From the Lassiter Ranch?"
"Yes sir I am."
'OK, then, and as I said, I hope it goes smooth for you."
"Thanks Sheriff, I'll talk to you later. Guess I better book a
room before there all gone." I said to him and left the
office. He waved at me as I left. I looked across

the street and saw Jeanie's Saloon and Hotel.
I walked over and went inside; it was bustling with cow
hands drinking and playing cards. Loud talking, laughter
and piano music in the background filled the room. You
could hardly hear you own thoughts and smoke was like
fog on the prairie. I walked up to the bar and the bartender
was a short chunky man, a little on the round side.
"Howdy, have a drink?" He said as he wiped the bar in
front of me.
"That sounds good." I replied
"Whisky or sarsaparilla?"
"Whisky," I answered, "looks like your pretty busy." He
nodded his head a set a glass down in front of me and
poured whisky into it.
"Two bits," he said, "From round here cowboy?"
"I'm Brad Lassiter, from the Lassiter ranch. I'm looking to
hire drovers for a drive. I'm going to need a room for a
couple of nights too!"
"We can fix that up. My names Mark, Mark Foor," he said
and reached out his hand to shake. "How many days you be
gonna' stay?"
"Staying until Sunday morning Mr. Foor. Going to try to
sign up some drovers here Sunday morning then I'll be
going back to the ranch to move our herd out Monday
morning."
"Where ya going, Abilene, Wichita?" He asked.

"No, St. Louis."

"Kidding me ain't ya? No body goes there anymore cowboy. Range's closed, Shawnee and Chisholm trails ain't been used for years I hear. All's fenced off or bought up by settlers. You ain't gonna' get there from here." He said with a frown on his face.

"My Dad and his men have figured out a trail, so they say. Don't know myself, but we are going." He looked at me with a bewildered look on his face. "Sounds mighty risky to me cowpoke, mighty risky. And rustler's, Injuns, mountains, I don't see it." He said. I thanked him and found a table to set at and looked around. Glen Berman and his Son Rhett were playing cards at a table not to far from me. Our eyes met, he sort of glared, and looked away. A lady came to the table.

"Hi stranger, I'm Kim Johnston. "You from round these parts?"

"Yes, was born not far from here. And you?"

"I'm from Dallas I'll be taking care of your table. Want to have something to eat? Foods real good here just like home." She said. "Just don't stiff me with your fare."

"Don't worry Miss Kim; I wouldn't do that to you!' She looked back and said. "I've heard that before, to many times. You can't trust a soul anymore around here. The pot roast is very good and made fresh today. Made from Elk, real tender, and tatters, carrots and onions. Smothered in gravy with biscuits on the side."

"That sounds real good, Miss Kim. And who do I see about a room for a couple of days?"

"I can handle that for you too. You all by yourself?" She quizzed.

"Yes, I am all by myself." I replied. "Just me."

"I can fix that up for you to, cowboy. Not I, but we got some pretty ladies workin' here. Miss Jeanie has brought some real cuties in. Mostly ladies from the East"

"No thank you, I'll be fine alone, just fine. But thank you for asking."

"I'll get your meal coming; it'll take a few minutes or so. Want another drink." She asked.

"No, I'll have coffee if you have some. Coffee will do just fine thanks"

"I'll get some made for you." She answered and walked to the bar. I heard Mark say in a loud voice, "Tell 'em four bits." She came back to my table and told me Mark was making coffee for me.

I asked her, "Why four bits for coffee and it's only two bits for whisky?

"He hates making it." She answered, "I told him to make it. I'm only going to charge you two bits." She shook her head and went to the kitchen.

I finished my meal and it was good. Kim gave me a key for my room and told me to pay Mark for the stay, and she collected the money for my meal and wished me a good stay. I carried my belongings to my room and put them on the bench at the foot of the bed. There was a pitcher with water in it and a bowl, so I washed up a little and then I started down stairs to get my horse boarded at the Livery Stable before it got dark. As I came down the stairs I glanced over at the table where Glen Berman and his son Rhett were playing cards. Glen looked at me with look of evil in eyes. I shook my head and ignored him. I got my horse and walked to the Livery to board her. There a man sitting on a stool outside the barn. "Howdy," he said, "Can I help ya?"

"I would like to leave my horse a couple of days if I can."

"Sure can," he answered, "four bits to board and another two bits if in' you want me to feed her. I got good hay and fresh oats."

"That will be fine sir; I'm stayin' till Sunday morn. You got a place with some shade for her to get out of the sun?"

"Sure do my boy, there's a lean- to on the side of the barn and water right handy. You can pay me when you pick her up. Nice look-in' filly you got here."

"Thanks, she's pretty alright, good ride too!"

"Don't worry about yer saddle. I'll take it off-in put it in the barn fer ya. Don't worry bout nuttin!" He said to me with a grin on his face.

"Again, thank you for your trouble; I'll see you Sunday morning." I shook his hand and his grip like to have broke my hand. As I was walking back to the Saloon I kept thinking about Mr. Berman. Why did he look at me like he did? I don't even know the man except of what I have heard. And what I heard wasn't all that favorable, that's for sure. I walked down the street and met Sheriff Royal walking the other way. He nodded his head and asked how I was doing and I told him all was OK. He still had that grin on his face. He told me to let him know if I needed any thing. It seemed like he wouldn't hurt a fly. Not like any law man I've seen before. I wouldn't want his job and especially in this town.

I pushed the swinging door's to enter the Saloon and as I stepped in I glanced over at Berman's table and he gave me one of those looks again. I walked over to Mark at the bar. "What's with him?" I asked. "If looks could kill I'd be dead."

"That's the way he is, not friendly or open to strangers." Mark replied. "Saw him looking at you poster when he came in and he pointed it out to his son Rhett. You might want to keep an eye on him. I just got a feeling, and it's not a warm and cuddly feeling either."

"Buy the boy a drink." Glen shouted to Mark. Mark grabbed a glass and poured a shot of whisky. I was surprised. I lifted the glass and turned to face him and he and Rhett were walking toward me.

"See yer planning a drive. Where ya going cowboy?" He said as he approached a grin on his face. "Need some drover do ya? Plenty around."

"My Dad has planned a cattle drive to St. Louis," I answered, "going to need a few."

"Has old Charlie lost his mind?" He blurted.

"I thought so myself at first, Mr. Berman, but he seems to have it all worked out."

"Sounds pretty nutsey to me son." He said. "You ain't gonna' get cattle all the way up there. Too many obstacles in the way, my boy, way to many."

"Like you!" Mark commented.

"Nobody asked for your opinion, tend your bar." Glen snapped back at him.

"You Lassiter's been running that ranch for years," Glen said, "knew your grandpa too! He was a Yankee supporter, wasn't he?"

"No Mr. Berman, he was a Texan. Didn't care much for, or about the war."

"He stopped selling cows to the southern cause, my boy."

"Well Mr. Berman, he didn't want to get paid with money that wasn't worth a damn is what I heard."

"Maybe if your grandpa had helped feed the troops we might have done better. That's the way I see it my boy." And he had that look in his eyes again. I had a feeling things were not well between us, and I slipped my hand into my vest pocket.

"Well let me say this Mr. Berman, the Lassiter's can take care of their business and you should tend to yours."

"Better be careful where you tread," Berman growled, "I was tendin' business when you were messin' yer pants sonny boy, and I just might take you over my knee, if I get a mind too!"

"I think I've heard all I want to hear from you Mr. Berman," and I stepped toward him my free fist clenched. His son Rhett pulled out a bowie knife and pointed it at me. When he did they heard the click of the derringer in my pocket being cocked. They both stepped back; surprise was the look on their faces.

"You thinking of bringing a knife to a gun fight?" I challenged.

Glen took his hand and pushed the knife down to Rhett's side.

The saloon was dead quiet. Glenn told his son to go back to the card table.

"And another thing Mr. Berman, I'm getting a little tired of that look you been given me." I told him with my hand still in my vest pocket. I was not sure if he had a weapon or not.

"Don't you worry none my boy." Mr. Berman whispered. "The way you're going you won't be seeing much of anything around here if you ain't careful." He turned and walked back to his table.

"I had ya covered, cowboy," Mark said to me, and gave me a glimpse of a sawed off double barreled shotgun he kept behind the bar. "There's trouble brewing now, for sure. Better keep your eyes wide open and look over your shoulder often. The Berman's don't cotton to being backed down much. And you can bet this ain't over by a long shot. Here have drink on me."

"Thanks anyway Mark, but I'll be hittin' the bunk. Had a long day and thanks for backing me up."

"You handled that well cowboy. Did you see the look on their faces? I got a kick outta that." Mark said with a grin. "You don't see the Berman's backing down none too often."

I thanked Mark again and went on up to my room and got ready for rest. I put the derringer under my pillow just in case. I figured they wouldn't try anything in the saloon, most likely to try to bushwhack me outside or from a side alley or some other secluded place. Had to get up early to telegram Miss Patti and let her know what's going on and ask Mark about where in town to get the rifles and ammo Dad wants me to get. How I was to get them back to the ranch without a cart or wagon. It was hard going to sleep as the noise from down in the saloon was constant and the ladies giggling going back and forth from the rooms down the hall. I wasn't asleep long when there was a knock on my door.

"Yes," I answered, 'who is it?"

"Mr. Lassiter, I need to see you." It sounded like Sheriff Royal.

I opened the door, and it was him.

"Sorry to bother you but I understand you pulled a pistol on Mr. Berman." He asked. "You know we have a no gun policy in town. I'll have to take it from you." I thought for a second. "No Sheriff, I didn't pull any pistol on him, I don't have one. He heard my tobacco can click when I put my hand in my pocket and he must have thought it was a derringer cocking." I reached in my vest pocket and pulled out my can of fixins' and showed it to him.

"Glen said you pointed a pistol at him"

"No Sir, I never pulled out a pistol. In fact they pulled a knife on me! You can ask the bartender, Mr. Foor, he was right there all the time. I just kept my hand in my pocket to make him think I had one"

"Alright, sorry for bothering you. I'll check with him and if he says what you say, it's forgotten. Good night." He turned and closed the door as he walked out.

Phew, quick thinking lad I thought to my self. Glen Berman or one of his men must have gone to the sheriff. He must have thought he was poking at a youngster that would be afraid of him. He didn't know of all my years on the range, rough towns and Indian fighting. I shook my head, said thank you Lord, and went back to bed.

Back at the Berman ranch, Glen Berman called his hands together.

"Look here men. We have moved back in and out of this territory for years, but this time we are going to stay. The Lassiter Ranch has been here for years and they think they are the king's of this here country. Well, they ain't no more." He said. "We are going to be the only number one in these here parts. I ain't moving no more." He pointed to the Dice twins and said; "You boys need a little exercise. Why don't you ease into town tomorrow and teach that Lassiter boy a lesson."

Chapter Six

  I spent the day looking around town, busy place. Mark told
me about a store were I could find the rifles Dad needed
and the ammo to go with them. I told the store owner I had
no idea how I was going to get them back to the ranch and
told me for two dollars he would take them to the ranch for
me. At least that was one thing off my mind. I next went to
the post office and sent a telegram to Miss Patti and told
her I would keep in touch with her as often as I could. I
went to the stable to check on my horse.
"Howdy cowboy, doing OK?" The owner asked.
"Just fine sir, just checking on my horse."
"She's fine. A stranger was here this morning and asked
about her. Wanted to know if she was fer sale and who the
owner was, I told him he'd have ta look ya up but I didn't
think she's fer sale.", he said to me.
"No she's not for sale, gonna' keep this one for a while.
What's he look like?"
"Sort of a rough one he was, he's seen some wear he did.
Looked like a gunslinger to me. Cold eyes, about six feet
tall he was. I didn't tell him where you was stayin, I just
told him yer in town fer a day or two."
"Well thanks; I'll keep an eye out." I waved bye at him and
started walking back to the saloon. About half way to the

saloon two young men came out of an alley and walked up to me.

"Think yer tough do ya?" One asked with a grin on his face.

"I can handle myself." I replied.

"Well let's see." He growled and made a move at me fists closed. I stepped back to protect myself from his advance and he took a swing at me. I ducked his swing but his partner had a club of some sort and it caught me hard on the left shoulder that diverted my attention from the first man who caught me with a hard punch to the side of my head. I stumbled back and got hit again with the club on my neck. It stunned me, glad he missed my head, it 'a knocked me out for sure. Again I got hit in the gut from his partner that bent me over. The other took a swing at me again with his club and I grabbed it and pulled it from him and took a swing at him but as I did the other one kicked me in the leg. By now there were quite a few men gathered around chanting and shouting. Not in anyone's favor, just over the excitement of the fight. Out of the crowd a tough lookin' man about six foot tall came into the fight and grabbed one of the young men. He turned him around and caught him up side the head with a punch that knocked him to the dirt. That gave me a chance to gather myself and I went to punching the other one. I hit him hard several times and bloodied his nose and cut him over the eye. He took a hard hit from my right jab to this jaw and went to the ground. He pulled out a knife and I kicked it away. The other man got up but the man that was helping me caught him again with a wicked punch to the head and knocked him out!

"That's enough." Came a command from behind me. It was Sheriff Royal with his pistol in hand. "What's going on here," he demanded, "how'd this get started?" The crowd all started telling him their versions and he told them to calm down speak one at a time. The man that helped me told the sheriff that I was attacked by these two and he came in to help me. Sheriff Royal listened to the others and asked for some help to take them back to the jail house. They both were banged up and bleeding pretty well.

I turned to the man that helped me and thanked him for coming to my aid.

"Looked like you needed a hand, partner." He said with a grin. "A fair fight is one thing I don't butt into, but that wasn't a fair fight as I saw it. Who were those men?"

"I don't know who they were, never saw them before. They came out of the alley and started a fight with me. Don't know why."

One of the men in the crowd came over and said.

"That was the twin brothers Cameron and Carsen Dice. They ride with the Berman outfit, thought they could take you out as it looked to me." He said. "Guess they found out different."

The man that helped me stuck out his hand and said; "Name's Matt Barnes, from Reno, glad to be of help to you. I think it's time for a drink, what do you think?" "It's a little early for drinkin', but yes, let's, I'm buying." I answered, and we walked to Jeanne's Saloon. As we walked into the saloon Mark said; "Heard there was excitement downtown.", with a grin on his face. "How about a shot of whisky boys."

I paid for the drinks and thanked Matt again for his help and asked him to sit at a table with me.

"What do you do here in town?" I asked.

"Just passin' through, lookin' for work. Got here last night. Is that your buckskin filly at the stable?"

"Yes it is but she's not for sale."

"Shame," he said, "she's really good lookin' horse, always liked buckskins."

"The man at the stable told me you were looking at her," I said, "Good to meet you. What type of work you lookin for?"

"Most any thing to make a dollar, as long as it's legal. Know anybody hiring?"

"You ever work with cattle?" I asked.

"Done some here and there, know someone that needs some help?"

I told him to come in Sunday morning and I could probably sign him up. He agreed to come in and check it out. We talked for a while about how the country was going and he seemed to know quite a bit about the plains and its going's on. We decided to join into a card game at one of the tables. I'm not a big card player but I enjoy a poker game once in a while. While we were playing, Sheriff Royal came in and asked if I wanted to press charges on the two men. I told him I wasn't going to but I did wonder what provoked it. He said he didn't know either but was going to fine them for breaking the peace and disorderly conduct. I agreed to that and he nodded and left.

We played cards for a while, won a little lost a little but broke even in the end. Matt went to see about a room and I went to the wash house to clean up before dinner. As I ordered dinner, Matt came and joined me. He was not much of a talker, always seemed like there was something else on his mind and he carefully watched customers come and go as we ate. Seemed restless. The rest of my stay in town was uneventful and quiet.

Sunday morning came and I went down to a table and Miss Kim brought coffee and served my breakfast. I set my papers on the table and got ready to take applications, I had no idea how many would show up to apply. Matt was the first to sit down and I took his information, asked about drives he was on and told him to check back with me at noon and that all looked good to me. I had quite a few men apply and some seemed OK and others I felt sorry for as I knew they needed work but they didn't have the experience. That would be like no help at all. So far Matt was the only one I would pick.

"Y'all lookin' for help," some one blurted out. I looked up and there was this tall lanky man of six foot four or more walking to my table with a bull whip looped over his shoulder. "Richard Witt," he said," most call me Mr. Witt amongst other things from time to time. Hear y'all lookin' for drovers. Where do I sign up?

"Right here Mr. Witt, where you from?" I asked.

"Florida, my man, the big state of Florida. Might not be as big as Texas, but big enough. Got a lot more cattle than Texas. 'He proudly exclaimed. "Bunch more from what I've done seen so far."

"I doubt that Mr. Witt." I answered; "A lotta' cattle here."

"He's a Cracker," Mark the bartender said loudly. "A Florida Cracker, get their name from the bull whip they use to herd cattle. I was down that way a long a while back, and he's right, they got cattle sure-nuff, and those Cracker horses can go all day I hear."

"Started when I was fifteen, during the war, ain't never stopped, 'cept for a spell." Witt said.

"How did you end up here?" I quizzed.

"After the war a lot of my family moved Northwest to join the Witt's that had been settled there for years to better themselves an start again. The war left a lot of the south in a mess. I stayed till ten years ago but heard some of my kin folk were having trouble in Wyoming, so I went to see if I could help-em out. We Witt's are a big family scattered all over this country, and we stick together through thick and thin. When a Witt's in trouble, us other Witt's jump in the ruckus. We Witt's are all over from Tennessee to California now. Anyway I got that tookin' care of, so now just driftin', doing what I can to earn a dollar. Saw yer sign an I figured I'd check 'er out."

"Well Mr. Witt looks you just might have a job, sign here and come back at noon."

"Have ta' put a W, I can read a little but not much on write-in'." He put an W on the paper and went to sit down. I went to bar to talk to Mark.

I looked back at the door and couldn't believe my eyes. Jeff Cushing who I served with in the cavalry fighting Indians walked in the door. Jeff was a tall good looking man with a mustache that came down his chin. Good with a gun too!

"Howdy brother," he said with a big grin on his face, "You need some help? I'm looking for some work."

"You been doing some cattle work?" I asked.

"Yeah, here in there, got pretty good at it I'd say."

"Well good to see you again Jeff, sign this paper, I think we can use you." I told him.

We talked over old times a little at the table, I shook his hand and we gave a hug to each other and he stepped back and sat down at a table and ordered coffee.

Time went by and this lady came in the saloon wearing a shirt and denim's. She had a nice figure, five foot two that filled out those denims nicely, long gold auburn hair appeared to be in her early twenties, a very striking good looking gal. She came over to my table.

"Can I be of any assistance to you cowboy?" She asked. I couldn't believe my ears. Is she trying to hit me up?

"I'm sorry young lady, your sure pretty enough, but I got a lot of work to finish and don't have time to play much. You're sure lovely though." She went red in the face and her eyes glared like burning embers.

"Lookie' hear you conceited idiot cow poke." She said in a voice of fire. "I ain't no lady of the night and I ain't given myself to no one but the right man and up to and including now I haven't seen any in these parts yet! Your lookin' for drovers ain't ya?""

"Yes ma'am I am, but you're a lady!" I replied.

"You might want to think that over a bit cowboy!" Mark the bartender proclaimed. "That's Amber Houston from the Houston ranch. Been driving cattle since the age of twelve. Heard that her Dad sent her out to bring back a stray cow and she came back with a Buff, two elk & a wolf."

"Not so," she said, "My Daddy made up that story. But I do know my stuff, that you can bank on. I can do the job."

I'm thinking to myself, I need drovers but if I sign her up Dad will have a raccoon crazy fit. Besides that, a woman on a drive?

That's gotta' cause problems I don't even want to start to imagine.

"You might want a listen to the bartender," a man sitting at a table said, "She been doing it for years, and I can vouch that she knows her stuff, I've rode with her. She's tough and can out shoot most men."

"Well ma'am sign here and check with me at noon," I told her, "No promises though."

"All I ask is you give me a fair shake and treat me as anyone else and hire me for my experience and nothing else!!" She proclaimed angrily. She signed and stomped off.

I sat there and shook my head in disbelief. The big problem was that I did not have the showing for applications I thought I would. I said that to Mark and he told me I wasn't going to get many locals as Glen Berman probably put the word of fear out to stay clear of ya."

I turned around and looked at the door and the biggest man I've ever seen walked in. He was built with the power of an ox. He was a black man, broad shoulders, and all muscle. At least six foot eight tall and his arms were bigger than my leg. I don't know where he found clothes to wear. He walked to the bar and asked Mark where the man was asking for drovers.

"That's me," I answered.

"I would like to sign up," he said.

Mark whispered in my ear that he worked for the Houston Ranch for several years and is a good honest man.

"Well sir I need drovers," I said to him, "but as big as you are, we wouldn't have any horses big enough to put under you."

"I have my own sir." He replied and he pointed outside. I went to the door and there were three of the biggest horses I've ever seen. They had the look of draft horses, not as heavy but well built and tall.

"If Miss Houston joins, I do too sir, if not, I will not. I've been watching over her for years and I go where she goes."

"What's your name?" I asked.

"Josh," he replied, "Josh, that's all."

"Mark says you have worked drives before."

"Yes sir," he replied, "several years for the Houston's." He was very polite and his speaking was perfect.

"Well Josh sign here," and I pointed where to sign. He leaned over the table and put an X where I had pointed.

"Come back at noon time Josh," I told him and as I looked at the clock on the wall. Noon would be in about forty minutes. I had a couple of good men and Josh could be one, but Amber, I just didn't know. Mark and the other man both said she had the experience, and experience I needed, but a woman? That could be awkward.

The time ticked by quickly and the clock struck twelve. Most of the men that I had spoken with came back in the saloon and stood there waiting. Amber came in with her hair under her hat. Now she looked like a young boy, a nice looking young boy at that. That gave me an idea. A little dirt smeared on her face I might may be able to pull it off for a while at least. Sooner or later Dad and the men would figure it out. But if she's as good as they say it wouldn't make a difference by then. Besides, we would be well into the drive and we couldn't just chase her off into the wilds.

 I picked up my papers and told them when I called off their name they could step forward, the rest could go. "Matt, Jeff, Witt, Josh, Trent Arthur and Andy step forward." Everyone started looking at each other in bewilderment. I pointed to Amber. She smiled, shook her head and stepped forward. Some of the other men were grumbling to each other. Some left and some went to the bar.

 I told them to gather their belongings and as soon as I got straightened out with what I owed the saloon we would meet at the stable. I went to the bar to settle my tab. "Thanks Mark for your help, and I enjoyed the stay."

"Good to have you cowboy, come back anytime," he said, "just wanta' ask ya, do you know that man Matt?"

"Matt Barnes? No I don't, he helped me out in that fight I got into with those men from the Berman outfit. Seems like an OK man. Why?"

"He looks awful familiar for some reason. Reminds me of a guy I saw when I was tending bar at a saloon in Reno a couple of years back. But the man I'm thinking of had a different name. Chuck Shoemaker it was. He was a gun slinger, an a good'in he was. I mean quick and deadly. He had gun fights in California, New Mex territory, Wyoming, Nevada, I mean he got around but suddenly dropped off the face of the earth."

"Well Mark there's a lot of guys out there that's looks like somebody else. Just a coincidence I suppose. Thanks for your help, got to get moving." I shook his hand and started for the stable, I'm sure he's got Matt mixed up with someone else. I hope!

I paid the man at the stable and picked up a piece of charcoal and went over to Miss Houston, or Andy I should say.

"Here, smear this on you face," I told her, "And try to keep clear of my Dad and Arnie the trail boss when we get to the ranch. Sooner or later they are going to figure it out, but I surely hope it's later, well into the drive."

"I will, and thanks for giving me the chance. I've been wanting to get out here and go east for quite a while. The money I make on this drive will do it and it's going to help Josh get on his own too!"

Well Dad told me to get drovers and I did. But when he finds out he's going to pitch a fit. The men all gathered at the corral, packed and ready to go. I asked the men to keep mum about Andy and they all agreed although I'm not sure if they agreed with my decision to hire her, him. "OK men lets move out." We rode off to the ranch.

Chapter Seven

We got to the ranch and it was bustling with activity.
Cookie was getting prepared to serve the evening meal for
the men. Carlon was getting all the horses herded up for the
start of the drive early Monday morning. Some of the men
had a large herd gathered just off the side of the ranch. Dad
and Arnie came riding in to meet the new hands.
"How'ed we do son," he asked as he got down from the
Dunn he was riding, got some good boys for us?"
"I got five, Dad, that's all I could sign up. But they are all
experienced."
"Good son, we could have used a few more, but that's a
help." I explained to him about Glen Berman warning
several not to sign and the others just didn't have
what it would take or the skills.
"Why the hell doesn't Berman mind his own business?
He's getting to where he thinks he owns everything around
here. Ain't nothing but trouble, he is." Dad exclaimed and
called the new men forward to address them.
"Gentlemen we are about to go on a big journey driving
thirty five hundred head of cattle to St. Louis. It's going to
be a hard tough drive, but we can do it. I want every one of
you to be on your toes and ready for anything, but you will
be well paid." He said and stepped forward to shake each

ones hand. When he got to Andy he took a hard look and asked. "How old are you boy?"

"Twenty two sir." She, or he replied

"Don't look a day over fifteen." He said. "You don't even look dry behind the ears yet." And turned and looked at me. I shook my head and told him. "He's got ten years on the trail, and I had it verified Dad." He looked back at Andy and said.

"Hope you got the strength to carry on son, you look a little puny." And he stepped back.

"I know I look young and small but my heart makes up for it sir. And I can handle a gun." She told him.

Dad stepped back and told them we would leave at day-break, after breakfast and gather up the rest of the herd being held along the trail as we moved forward heading due north. He looked at Mr. Witt and asked. "Are you any member of the Witt's in Wyoming?"

"Yes sir, we are related. I just spent some time with them helping out with some problems they had and then worked my way down to this area."

"Good bunch of people," Dad replied, "Bought some cattle from a John Witt in Seventy six, good strong honest bunch, my man. Glad to have you. "

"Thank you sir, that was my Grandfather. We Witt's try to do right, but don't like being cheated or stepped on." Dad shook his hand and stepped back.

"Any question, men?" He asked. They all looked at one another and waved to say all was OK. Dad told them to get a bunk and get ready for the evening meal and get settled in. He came to me and said "That's the biggest man I ever saw, black or white." Speaking of Josh. He then told me he wanted me to distribute the rifles and fifty round of ammo to the men that didn't have rifles including me. I told him I would take care of it, he patted me on the back and said he had a lot to do and would see me at dinner. I put my horse in the corral and saw a smaller horse not fourteen hands with a wavy mane and tail. I asked Carlon about it.

"That's a Welsh, they say. They come from England from what I hear. They got a big chest and a body that tappers back. Not like our horses and if you don't put a Martindale on him your saddle will slide back and drop ya! They say they are hardworking an' got spirit. At least that's what I'm told. Don't know much about 'em." Carlon told me.

"He's a good lookin' boy." I said. "Well built."

"Yea and he's a feisty little devil too! And when you put your foot in the stirrup you better be ready to ride." Carlon answered.

"I'll have to give him a try, Carlon, looks like he's got heart. Talk to you later, gotta' get my stuff ready."

I went to the men and distributed the rifles then started packing what I was going to need. I know one thing; it's going to be a hot drive. At about five John rang the dinner bell and the men began lining up for chow, plates in hand. John had a small hog on a spit and started carving and serving. There was a pot of beans and a pot of cabbage next to the fire, the men helped themselves to that. And of course there was a big pot of coffee. All dug in and sat around talking and laughing. John started packing up to take meals to the men further up the trail that were holding cattle. We also had twelve Mexican cowboys Dad hired, they called themselves Vaqueros. They wore big sombreros' and clothing with a lot of silver Conchos on them. They were up the trail with the other men waiting to be fed. As soon as the plates were washed he headed out. He had a long night ahead of him. I wouldn't want his job; it took a special man to do it.

Cookie as we called John was the best there is when it came to running a chuck wagon. He had a four mule team pulling a good size wagon and a smaller one behind that one. It had beans, dried meat, coffee, and some fresh and dried vegetables, water barrels, sugar and grains such as rice, corn and oats. There were potatoes, onions, salt and spices. And somewhere in there was always some whisky and wine, they were just in case items. Some of the cow hands carried there own whisky in their belongings.

Cookie was also the dentist, barber and doctor. It was a demanding job and you didn't give Cookie any guff and didn't touch his things unless you were told. The chuck wagon man made about thirty dollars a month plus the men gave him favors when they could such as bullets, tobacco and if they had a chance to get a deer or a hog that was always welcomed. Some times Cookie would take his Indian woman with him but this time he left her home to take care of running the moonshine still. So he was making income at home while he was on the trail. Steve Lowery, the blacksmith had a small wagon with a small forge, coal and horse shoeing supplies to keep the horses feet taken care of on the drive pulled by one horse. He got his gear together and when John left he followed behind him.

Dad, Steve and I went to the wash house to get ready for dinner. Mom rang the bell while we were washing so we were right on time. Mom made a great dinner as always and was putting it on the table as Dad poured us a shot and we sat down to eat, it was really good. I was thinking, Cookie does a good job but we would miss Moms meals. We ate our dinner, had coffee and we helped Mom clean up, much to her protest. We then had a night cap and talked a little about starting the drive in the morning and then decided to hit the sack. A million things ran though my head but I was finally able to sleep.

Back at the Berman ranch, Glen had called his outfit together again. "Boys, the Lassiter outfit is starting off tomorrow morning on a cattle drive." He told them. "Well we are going to see that all them cattle don't make it. I want you boys to get with our Injun friends and follow them for a couple of days. When they get three or more days away from any towns I want those cattle stampeded and scattered. We will round up all we can and bring 'em back to our ranch. I want you to dress as Injuns so they don't have any reason to suspect us. And if any of 'em get shot. Too bad! Got that?" He asked. The men nodded their heads in approval.

Chapter Eight

 It wasn't daybreak yet and Steve hollered in the door;
"Rise an' shine brother!"
I got out of bed and put on my clothes. As I was setting into
my boots I thought to myself about how I was going to
miss that soft bed. Went downstairs and Mom had biscuits
and gravy ready on the table. Dad and Steve sat down and I
joined them.
"Boys we start this morning on the drive of our lives. It's
going to be hard and tough but we will get it done." He
said. "Making more money than we have ever seen. Let's
get saddled up and move em' out."
 We all gave Mom a hug and she wished us well. She held
Dad warmly and told him to be safe and careful. He gave
her a kiss and told he loved her and not to worry.
 We got saddled up and joined the men waiting for us.
"Men," Dad said, "We are going to take what we have here
and head due north.
We will meet with the others holding cattle along the way.
By the time we past Nacogdoches we should have all thirty
five hundred head together. OK boy's lets get-em moving.
RO-L-L-L-L 'EM Out"
 Most of the men waved their hats and hollered "Yahoo"
and we started off. As the morning went on the heat started
to build up and with the lack of rain the dust was pretty bad

and there was not much of a wind to help with the dust. If we could get a west or east breeze that would be a plus for us. The area was brushy and mostly flat so we were going at a good pace. I kept an eye on Amber and she seemed to know what to do. I was glad to see that. I guess those men knew what they said about her. We stopped for nooner where John had left some coffee and some sort of tortillas with beans and chopped meat. He wrapped them in paper and buried them in the sand to keep them cool and away from bugs. They were tasty and hit the spot. Babe seemed to be doing well so I didn't change my ride like some did. "How's your ride doing?" I asked Mr. Witt.

"One thing about these Cracker horses," He said, "They mostly can go all day unless it really get super hot and in need of water."

We had a few small streams from time to time so we had water for the stock. We traveled at a good rate before it was time to gather the herd at let them graze. John had picked out a good spot with water and grass for the stock to feed on. He had our dinner and coffee ready so we split into two groups so one half could eat and the other half stayed with the cattle. After the first group ate they would take over and let the other half come in and get their fixin's. Dad told the men that we would split up into two groups. One group would sleep until twelve thirty and relive the men watching the herd and the second group could sleep until day break, about six in the morning. We sat around the fire as it was cooling off a little and talked of old times and past drives. Amber got her blanket and crawled under Cookies wagon. I put my saddle blanket over my saddle as a pillow and snuggled in until they called to switch crews.

I swear it didn't seem like five hours as when we were called to relieve the crew on with the herd. I saddled up and Amber rode out with me.

"Beautiful night," she said, "sleep well sir?"

"Yes I did, didn't seem that long though." I answered.

"You can call me Brad, we aren't that formal, Amber, everyone calls each by first names or nick names."

"Didn't want be rude or disrespectful, and I don't know the men that well. My Daddy always taught me to respect others. Gotta' relieve my man," she said, "talk to you later."

"Be careful." I told her as she rode off. She waved back to me.

The night was quiet except a coyote cry every so often. The air was cool and felt good but I knew come morning that would change. It's been so dry and hot and made for dusty conditions. And the lack of a west or east wind made you wear your bandanna across your face to kept from eating dirt. But it got into your eyes. As the sun rose we rode to the camp and got some coffee and eats. After we got our meal Cookie packed up and went on out to set up our nooner'. Steve the Blacksmith was not far behind him by the time we got the herd moving north again.

Three days out we were north of Lake Murval and west of the town of Carthage and we had all the cattle now and the twelve Mexicans. AK the Sioux drover rode up to me. "We got warriors watching us." He advised. "Been seeing 'em for a couple of hours on both sides of us. I don't like it."

"How many AK?" I asked.

"Don't rightly know." He answered. "Maybe fifteen, twenty. They tryin' to stay out of sight seems like. Swear they're up to no good. Look like a mixed up bunch of renegades. Toting rifles they are."

"OK, let's warn the men to keep an eye out and be ready just in case there is trouble." I said to him.

"I tell you, trouble is in them, Mr. Brad. An Indian knows an Indian. I bet they make a move just after dark.", he responded and galloped off. We better be on our toes I thought, and under the cover of dark we will be hard pressed to keep the herd together. I rode up to Andy and told her of what was coming down.

"Got my rifle and pistol loaded, Brad. I'll keep my eyes and ears open.", she said.

I tipped my hat and went on to warm the ones up front. AK and Dad came riding up to me.

"Brad, AK said the best way to handle this is don't act like we are aware of them following us." Dad pointed north west." Up the trail just a bit more there is a curved rock ridge wall that runs for a mile or so. He suggests that we pull up the herd early when we get to the ridge and just before dark we push the cattle up against it as tight as we can. And soon as it gets dark spread the men on the outer edge of the herd and we might surprise them."

"Sounds like a good idea Dad. That should work."

"AK is going to ride to Cookie," Dad continued, "And have him set up at the far end of the herd close to the end of the ridge wall and make it look like the men are getting ready to have their meal. Let's get moving and tell the men." He went one way and I the other. We had to get too them quickly so we could get this plan into action. Not only was AK a good drover but he was a crafty warrior. When I told Amber, she didn't act like she was real worried, and nodded her head. "I'll be ready." She said. This whole thing had me very concerned for her safety, and the safety of the men. It worried me. But AK's plan sounded good. I've been ambushed many times by Indians in the open country while on drives and in the cavalry and I knew it could get messy. Not to mention the dangers involved.

The men slowly moved to the westerly side of the cattle and started to move them at a easy rate, not too fast, toward the ridge wall. At least that would give us an advantage.

They couldn't hit us from the east side, it was too high. John had his wagons in position to block the north end and was starting to make a fire for the evening meal. Steve Lowery the blacksmith moved his wagon in line with Cookies. The sun was going over the horizon and it would be dark soon. He put some barrels and boxes around the fire with blankets on them and a hat here and there to make it appear men were sitting around the fire waiting to eat. I thought that was a clever move. It got dark and it looked like a dozen men were sitting around the fire and Cookie John was busy making like all was normal. He had two pistols stuck in his belt and one new-fangled Christopher Spencer slam fire shotgun that held five shells leaning against one of the barrels close by. He was ready.

Chapter Nine

I rode around to the west side of the herd near Amber. A K and my brother Steve rode up and told me they were going to ride out further from the herd and split up. That way they could tell how many warriors were coming to hit us. Two drovers were on the outside with Amber and I and Howard Brandon just a little south of them. The rest of the men were on their horses just inside the herd and were laying forward on the horses necks to blend in with the cattle. We waited.

It seemed like forever, I guess because of the anxiety and tension and it was dead quiet. I was thinking they would try to sneak in and hit us at close range. Suddenly I could hear horses coming on a hard run right for our center. They let out a bunch of hootin' and war cries and were coming hard. Amber threw up her rifle and shot one right off his horse. Our men came charging out and all hell broke loose. The night was lit up with rifle fire. One was so close he was but only fifteen feet from me when I shot him with my pistol and he hit the ground on his back. A couple more braves fell and the others turned and headed out as fast as they came in. I heard A K and Steve fire as they ran past them. It was over and over fast. The cattle were spooked some, but were under control. A K came riding in and when he got close to us one of the braves that was laying on the ground jumped up and leaped on his horse. A K shot him and he went back down. Then A K got off his mount, knife in hand and went to scalp him.

"A K, I wish you wouldn't." I hollered. He ignored me, but said.

"Boss, better have a look at this." As he pointed at the dead Indian. "This ain't no brave, it's a white man." I got off my horse and walked to him. He was right it was a white man dressed as a brave.

"What the hell." I said. "That is a white man alright. What's going on?"

"Looks like they trying to blame injuns for this raid." A K answered and went to get the man's horse." Got the Berman brand on him he does."

"Were they all Bermans?" I asked him, my mind in a puzzled set.

The men went and checked the others and they were Indians and Indian ponies.

I turned to Amber and said; "Good shootin' Andy." She nodded her head and wiped her brow.

"Better tell your Dad Mr. Brad." A K said. I waved at him and rode to find my Dad. Arnie got the men to spread out the cattle to graze and told them to keep their eyes and ears open. Dad was at Cookie's wagon talking with him and Steve Lowery.

"How many went down?" He asked.

"Four I know of." I answered. "But there's a problem Dad. One of those warriors was a white man."

"A white man?" He asked.

"Yes Dad a white man on a horse with the Berman brand on it. The rest were Indians."

"What the hell is going on?" Dad replied. "Think the Bermans started this or was he just riding with them?"

"I don't know Dad but it any way or form we got lucky. Not one of our men got hurt. A K's plan worked just as he thought it would"

"Ole John wounded one but he got away." Dad said. "Don't know what to think of it."

A K came riding up, two scalps in hand. Dad just shook his head and said something about how we just can't get him out of that practice.

"Throw that white man over his horse and let him go. He'll find his way back." Dad ordered.

"No sir," A K said, "bury him here and let the horse go. That way if the Bermans did have anything to do with this they won't know if we got him hostage or if he's dead and they will be out lookin' for him. Then you'll know for sure."

"If it is the Berman outfit what's going on with that man?" Dad growled. "He's been nothing but a trouble maker since he's came back to this territory. Round up the Indian ponies and give 'em to Carlon. Might be able to use em.'"

"Soup's on, grab a plate." John bellowed, with a grin on his face.

We gathered around had coffee and swapped stories of our side of the battle as Cookie filled our plates. Some of the men watched the cattle and waited for someone to relieve them so they could eat. After eating we buried the dead and went back to camp and had some more coffee. John brought out a whisky bottle and offered us a drink. The men split up, some to nap and other to take their shift with the herd. I laid my blanket and rolled into it. But I knew I would sleep light because of the chance they might return. Amber got her blanket and crawled under Cookies wagon and Josh slept near by.

Glen Berman was furious when Rhett and the men rode into camp and Rhett told him what had happened.

"Dad we were ambushed!" He proclaimed. "Just like they knew all along we were coming."

"Ambushed?" Glen shouted, "We were supposed to be the ones doing the ambushing. What the hell went wrong?"

"Dad, it was like they knew. We were the ones surprised. When we rode in they were waiting for us and they had the herd up against a high ridge wall. We never got close."

"How many men did we lose?" Glen demanded.

"We lost four men. Three Indians and Steve Spurrier's dead or missing." Rhett answered. "Eathon Gallo, Billy King and one of the Dice twins wounded. But not serious."

"That's not what I wanted." He bellowed. "I'm gonna' get aholt of Ron Hargrove, Bob McLenden and LaDon Drawdy and we will hit 'em again. And this time full force with Ron's and our men in broad daylight. I know of a good spot where they have to go through a valley and we will be waitin' on 'em. Get them wounded patched up while I ride and get the others in here. I wanta get this over and get all of that herd I can get. Now get busy." Glen went out, got on his horse and rode off.

That night I had the second shift and when supper was dished out I got a plate full, some coffee, and sat down with Mr. Witt.

"Doing OK Mr. Witt," I asked.

"Fine young man, doing just as fine as frog hair, and you?"

"Doing good, Mr. Witt, but it sure has been hot!"

"Yea-buddy, it's been that, Mr. Brad. Reminds me of down Florida way. Only so more humid down there. On a hot day the air is like breathing water. We got so much more rain, seems like to me. We could use a drizzle or two more here."

"We'll get some I'm sure Witt, but I hope it's in the day time though." I answered. "What's that gun you got? A cap and ball? It's got a brass frame".

"It was a cap and ball." Witt replied. "It's a copy of the Remington army model.

The South didn't have the iron the North had so people donated brass bed frames and such to help the war effort. And where ever they could use brass in place of iron it got put there. An old gunsmith in Ohio changed it to a 44 cartridge gun. Did a bang up job he did. Shoots good." I asked him if he fought for the South and he told me he didn't actually join but drove cattle for a rancher down there to Hogtown, Florida. After the war he said he stayed for a time but decided to ease west. We talked for a while and I bid him good night. I rolled a smoke, took a sip of coffee and hit the blanket to get some rest before my morning shift.

The next morning after eating I saddled up the Welsh horse, he was a little feisty at first but calmed down shortly. I saw Amber outside of the herd on the right front and I rode up to her.

"That sure was good shootin' last night Amber." I said to her.

"Thanks, wasn't much, he was right in my face so to speak. Hard to miss when it's like that." She replied.

"Your family owned the Houston ranch for years, didn't they?" I asked.

"Yes we did. But when Daddy died, Josh and I with help from the few men we had tried to keep it going. I was getting behind on a loan Daddy had taken from the bank to keep the ranch going. But the last two winters were very severe. We lost some cattle from the deep freezing snows both years. It was tough. And buying feed and hay to keep the herd healthy and alive hurt our money supply."

"So you lost it to the bank?" I asked.

"Well yes and no." She said. "The bank was pushing me pretty hard and I was catching up but not fast enough for them and they kept pressuring me to pay or sell. And Mr. Berman was dogging me to sell the ranch to him and I wouldn't sell especially to him and his bunch."

"Berman wanted your ranch?"

"Yes, he was really pushing me to sell, but what he was offering was far below the real worth. And even if he did offer more I wouldn't sell it to him. And I told him so to his face. He was furious."

"So what happened?"

"One day I rode into Lufkin to buy some goods we needed. The men were out gathering up some of the herd to take to market." She answered. " With the money we got from the cattle I could finally see myself getting out of debt. There was no one watching the ranch. When I returned the house, bunkhouse and the barn were on fire"

"How'd that get started?"

"It was very suspicious to me. The men saw the smoke, but it was too late to do anything about the fires when they got there. All the buildings burnt to the ground. One of the men rode into town and got the sheriff to come out and look at what happened. The sheriff said that the house burning must have set the barn a fire and spread from there. I didn't buy that story at all. I believe they were intentionally set all at the same time."

"So what happened then?" I asked.

"We drove most of the cattle to market and sold them. I paid the men and gave them the few cattle that was left and said to hell with it."

"You just let the ranch go?" I asked her.

"Yes, I saw no way of starting again. It would have taken all the money we made to rebuild the house, barn and other buildings with furnishings. And if I paid the mortgage off, we wouldn't have money for the buildings. So Josh and I left."

"So what happened to the ranch after that?" I questioned.

"Glen Berman went to the bank and bought the deed for what I owed and moved in on the property. If you want to know, I think it was his outfit that set it a fire. There were several horse tracks all over the grounds. But it couldn't be proven as Glen and his son Rhett, by all accounts were playing cards in Jeanne's saloon."

"I am so sorry, Amber. That's a real shame."

"Thanks Brad but it's done and over. With the money I have and the money I make on this drive I will go back east and try to find me a small farm. Josh will most likely stay somewhere here in the western territory, not sure."

I told her again how sorry I was about her loss, and tipped my hat and rode toward the back of the herd. There was a west breeze today so the dust wasn't bad at all. But it was hot. The sweat was just running down my back and the seat of my pants was soaked. We are making good time and we were nearing the west side of the town of Marshall, a couple of miles to the east. Then it came to me if the Bermans torched her ranch what would stop them from burning ours? That was worrisome to me so I road to find my Dad. When I found him I told him about what "Andy" had told me and that I was afraid for Mom's safety as there were not too many men at the ranch with her. I suggested that I ride into Marshall and telegraph Sheriff Royal to keep a lookout on her and the ranch. He agreed with me, and worried if that cowhand we shot was from the Berman outfit and Glen was the mastermind of that attack what's to keep him from trying to burn us out?

I switched horses and saddled up Babe for the ride into town. I checked with the men to see if they needed anything. Most of the men wanted fixins' for smoking or some candy. Matt Barnes offered to ride into town with me so we watered up and headed east. We made town in a little over an hour. As we rode in town I asked a man on the boardwalk where the telly office was? He pointed out a little store with red porch posts to me and wished me a good day. Seemed like a quiet little town. But then I noticed something that bothered me a little. There were several horses with the Berman brand tied to the rail in front of the saloon. I pointed it out to Matt and he told me he had seen them also. Why were they up this way? They couldn't be pushing cattle as there was no stockyards close in this area. Unless they were buying cattle, maybe, or just stealing them.

I went in and sent my telegram asking for Mom's safety to Sheriff Royal. Nice little store it was and they had smoking supplies and candy. I got what the men asked for, paid the clerk and asked him how business was?

"Picking up every day." He said. "An old prospector found some silver up in the hills near by and miners have been coming in every day. Don't know how long it's gonna' last, but I reckon it'll bring some money in."

I thanked the clerk and I asked Matt if he wanted to get a drink before leaving town. He thought it was a good idea. I noticed that Matt had lowered his pistol belt and tied the holster with leather thong around his leg. Did he expect trouble? I hadn't seen him wear his gun like that before now. We walked into the saloon and went to the bar and ordered a drink of whiskey.

"You boys from around these parts?" The bartender asked.

"No, just passin through." I told him. "I had to send a telegram back home."

"Understand you boys had a little trouble with some Injuns." A cowpoke at the near table blurted out.

"How'd you know about that?" I replied.

"News travels fast in these parts cowboy. Specially bad news. Don't take long atoll." He answered.

"You boys wouldn't know anything about that would ya?" I asked.

One of them stood up with a threatening posture, hand at his side answered.

"You accusing us of having anything to do with that?" He growled.

"No I ain't accusing you of nothing. Just asking but one of those Indians was a white man riding a horse with the Berman brand." I said to him.

"Better mind what ya say partner. Pointin' fingers can get ya in a heap of trouble. We lose horses to Injuns' here and there. He musta' been a half breed" He said very surly.

"I think there's more to it than that fella'. So why don't you shut up and set down and get your hand away from that pistol." Matt told him. "You seem mighty touchy."

"Touchy enough to handle what comes my way pard." He told Matt. The saloon went silent and men standing were backing up. This didn't look good at all. Another man at the table stood up with his hand by his gun.

"I'm a thinking you better do the shuttin' up.", he said to Matt. "Your mouth just might get you in a heap of trouble my friend."

"Don't want trouble," Matt said, "So if you know what's good for you, better take that hand off your gun and sit down. And you ain't no friend of mine either. Now sit down and shut up and we'll be leaving."

"You ain't telling me ta shut up." He bellowed and pulled on his gun. It never got it out of his holster. Matt got him dead center in the chest and the man went over backward like he was kicked by a mule. I had my gun out pointed at the other man just in case. But he put his hands up and he backed away. He sat down looking at the man on the floor.

"That was pretty darn fast cow poke, I mean deadly fast!" The bartender said. "But fair and square, no doubt about it, fair and square. He went for his pistol; you had no choice as I see it"

I paid for our drinks and the bartender told the rest of them at the table to drag their man on the floor out of his saloon. "Wait a minute." I said. "Let us get out first so we can head out of town without being shot at." The bartender agreed and put a double barrel coach gun on the bar.

"Good idea, you boys head on out I'll see you're not followed." Matt and I backed to the door of the saloon. Matt paused to look outside before we stepped out. We got on our horses and rode out of town not letting any grass grow beneath our horse's feet. A couple of miles out of town we slowed to a trot then stopped and looked behind to see if we were being followed. All looked to be clear.

"That was some fast shootin'." I said to Matt.

"Just lucky, I just got lucky." He replied.

"I'll say this, Matt, damn good luck then."

He nodded his head and we moved on. As we were riding I kept thinking about what Mark the bartender said in Lufkin when he questioned me about Matt. Chuck Shoemaker? I don't know, but fast, fast as lighting he is!

Chapter Ten

When Glen Berman got the news at his camp he was furious.

"What the hell is going on?" He asked. "Are we going to let the Lassiters stomp all over us? What is going on? Can't you men do anything right?"

"That cowpoke was super fast Glenn. Pete didn't even get his pistol out of his holster." One answered. "I ain't never seen nuttin' like it."

"What's Old Charlie doing, hiring gun slingers for drovers?" Glen questioned.

"Seems like it, he was fast calm and cold." Was the reply from one of his men.

"Well boys as soon as Ron Hargrove and his men get here were movin' out." Glen said. "We gotta get around that herd and into that valley to set up. And things will be different this time boys. I guarantee it."

"I hope so Dad," Rhett said, "They got us dead to rights last time."

"Somebody or someone tipped them off. Other wise they wouldn't of had no idea we were coming. And if I find out who it was, he's a dead man." Glen declared.

Matt and I found the trail of our herd and were riding to catch up. They were making good time as we were north of the Town of Caddo Lake. We decided to stop and make camp and ride out in the morning. Matt started a fire and walked into a wooded area a few yards away. I put some coffee makings on and got my fix-ins out to roll me a smoke. Wasn't to long and Matt came back with a rabbit. He had taken a forked stick and sharpened the ends which if you stuck it into a hole and could feel the rabbit you poked it up against the critter and twisted it. It would wrap up in its skin and fur and you could pull dinner out. It was an old Indian trick. Had to be careful though as that hole just might have a rattle snake hiding in there. Which was good eat in' too, you just had to handle that with a lot more care and respect. While the rabbit was roasting we rolled us a smoke and pored us a drink of whisky. It was so nice to relax and it wouldn't be long before I was ready to roll up in a blanket.

We poured coffee and started on the rabbit, it was very good. We cleaned up our plates with hot water and set the coffee pot next to coals to be warm in the morning. Matt and I checked on the horses and we both got our rifles and crawled into our blankets. It was quiet for a while then the coyotes started talking to each other. I woke up a couple of times to put some sticks on the fire but Mat had beat me to it the second time. We didn't want the fire too big as to attract any attention in case there were Indians passing by. A coyote had come in camp smelling around for something to nibble on, didn't stay long. Around four in the morning I heard the heavy sound of horses and I went to tell Matt but he heard them also and was awake. We sat there, rifles ready, but who ever they were road out of hearing distance quickly.

We awoke at day break and had a quick cup of coffee, saddled up and hit the trail. We came across the tracks of the riders we heard. They went north following our herd them moved off to a north easterly direction. We could tell they weren't Indian horses as they all had shoes on their feet. We got up with the herd around noon just in time for lunch. The men all came to get their goodies and I gave Amber some rock candy. She really liked that and thanked me, her face blushing. I told her to rub some more charcoal on her face. She smiled and rode off. We drove on making good time and we were at the north end of Texarkana Lake. Cookie had got set up and there was plenty of pasture for the herd to eat and settle down.

Matt and I decided to take the second shift to catch up on rest. I rolled a smoke and hit the blanket shortly after. As I was wrapping the blanket over me I saw my brother Steve and A K with their rifles and a blankets heading out of camp to sleep out there and listen for trouble. They split up and headed in different directions. They did this every night. I knew we could sleep well and not worry. Nothing could get by those two.

After taking our shift we had breakfast and started moving the herd out. We were now moving on a northeast direction west of the City of Texarkana and would soon move more easterly facing the cattle toward Little Rock Arkansas. A K had laid out a good trail just as Dad said he would. So far we didn't run in to any fenced up range or run over anyone's crop land as far as I could tell. That's good...

We rode on pushing the cattle and making good time and we were a couple of days northeast of Texarkana. The weather was hot but I could feel a chill in the air and the breeze was picking up. That was nice but it meant one thing. Rain was a coming. Now there is nothing to compare to riding a horse in a rain storm. Even with your slicker on you still got wet all the way to your toes and chilled to the bone. And if you didn't have chaps on your legs your boots filled with water and your toes shriveled up. It must be July by now. But what day I do not know and won't find out unless we meet someone or go into a town we pass by. The rain hit us late in the afternoon and continued well into the night. When a hard rain comes down it makes it hard on Cookie John to prepare the meal for the men. He can only carry so much dry wood in one of his wagons and the men would gather
what wood they could find and pile it close to the fire to dry. John had a good sized tarp with tall poles he put over the fire to keep the rain from drowning it. He had to keep

the fire down some so the tarp wouldn't catch fire. The cattle were being restless and belligerent and that didn't help things any. It was just plain miserable for all of us to say the least. It was hard to keep your fixins' dry so you could roll a smoke. I kept mine in a leather pouch inside a tin under my hat. But when it's raining hard, forget it! Some men carried a pipe to alleviate that problem. By morning the rain had stopped and the rising sun was making it very humid. And the sweat started running down my back again. But I was already wet from the rain.

 We were west of a town called Hope so Don Volsch and James Harrell rode into town to get some supplies for Cookie and odds and ends for some of the men. When they caught back up with us they told my Dad that they saw horses with the Berman brand on them and several horses with brands they didn't recognize with them. They said it was a good sized group. Why were the Berman this far north?

I'm sure they weren't going for cattle and I'm sure they weren't leaving Texas after getting the Houston Ranch site. What were they up to, I was thinking. And I'm sure whatever it was; well it's probably not good. At least I found out it was July 7th.

 Ron Hargrove had brought his men to meet the Bermans and they were riding hard North East. It was about five days ride between Hope and the next town of Arkadelphia and there was a narrow valley on the trail right in the middle. That's where Glen Berman was setting up his men for an ambush on the herd.

"OK men," Berman said, "I want Ron and his men to set up on the east side and we will put us on the west side. When that herd gets in the middle we will open up on them and we should be able to get at least half the herd. If anybody gets in the way well that's just a shame, if you get my message."

They went to get set up. It was a perfect spot with plenty of cover and with the herd stretched out our men would be a hard pressed to protect themselves or the herd.

A K always rode ahead of the herd to look out for danger or Indians that may be a threat to us. About mid day right after our nooner' A K came riding back to us on a hard run.

"Stop the cattle!" He hollered. "There's danger ahead. Several men in the valley ahead. Many more than our numbers I fear an ambush." My Dad came riding up to see what all the fuss was about and A K told him what he saw ahead.

"What ya reckon we do?" He asked. A K told him he knew of a band of Sioux and Comanche camped not far from us and figured if we gave them a couple of steers they would help us. They would never turn down a fight. He told me to take some of the men and get on top of the east side of the valley and he would get the Indians and get on the opposite side. He had a mirror and would flash it when he was in position. On the second flash we would make our move.

"Now ride," he said, "We meet in two hours." I got Jeff Cushing to ride with us as he and I knew the country from our cavalry days. I got Don Volsch, Buddy Perryman, Matt Yeaton, Arnie Arnold, Lee Tingy, Joe Parmer, Howard Branden, Matt Barnes and my brother Steve. The rest of the men and my Dad would stay with the herd. Andy offered to go with us but I told her to say with the herd. We watered up got on fresh horses and made sure all had rifles and they were fully loaded and we started out. When we got to the valley entrance we headed east and then north up to the top off the rim. Before we got to the rim looking down into the valley I told the men to spread out and stay from the edge as not to be seen. Steve and I snuck to the edge to scope it out. We could see them hiding amongst the rocks below us and they were not looking up our way. They were concentrating on the southerly direction the herd was approaching from. I hoped A K was able to get enough of those Indians to help us or if he got any at all as the camp may have moved. If he didn't we wouldn't be able to pull this off. I gave Jeff a signal to spread the men out along the edge and lay down as not to tip anyone off. We waited.

The sun was beating down on us and I was glad we had filled the canteens, it sure
was hot. About thirty minutes went by and I was wondering where A K was. Suddenly I saw a flash. I hoped he was not alone. Steve signaled Jeff to move the men up for the ready. I had my man in sight and was ready to pull the trigger. Come on flash again I thought. Then it came. I gave the signal and all hell broke lose as the men started firing down on them. That's when I found out what took so long for the second flash. Not all the Indians had rifles and had to sneak in closer among the rocks to get a shot with their bows. We opened up. I hit the man
I was watching, and wounded him. He was holding his shoulder trying to get to his horse. Most of the men below us were scrambling to get to their horse but several were not moving at all. We were successful. A K again saved the day. I didn't care what side he was on at the Little Big Horn. If he was on our side it may have been different I thought to my self. The men that got away were heading south out of the draw toward where our cattle were being held. I hollered at our men to mount and get back to where the herd was waiting. I signaled A K to run south and mounted up. I'm sure he had to get a scalp or two first.
We rode hard to get back to where our men were holding the herd. When we got there it was a sight to see as our men were waiting in position as Glen Berman, his son

Rhett who was wounded pretty good, and Ron Hargrove with a couple of his men rode up face to face about thirty yards apart from our men. It was a stand off. Glen got off his horse.

"Charlie," he bellowed, "Step out here and let's get this over between you and me right now!" As my Dad started forward Mat Barnes got off his horse and walked between them facing Glen.

"Gonna' shoot an old man?" Matt asked Berman. "He's no gun fighter"

"Ain't no older than me!" Glen said with a surly look on his face. "So get out of the way I'm fixin' to finish this out here and now."

"Better step back Berman," Ron Hargrove said. "I know that man and he's quicker than a rattlesnake and twice as deadly. Get on your horse and let's head for home. I've had enough of your nonsense anyway. I ain't kidding, you're looking at death, eye to eye, and it's the last thing you're ever gonna' see." Glen went for his gun. Matt drew and hit him in the right shoulder before he had a complete grip on his pistol. It staggered him and almost turned him around as he held his arm.

"Coulda' killed ya," Matt said, "But I don't kill old men."

"Dad," Rhett shouted, "Stop please. Now we both need help. We gotta' get to the town of Hope and see a Doctor as quick as we can." Glen staggered to his horse and one of Ron's men helped him get up in the saddle.

"Mr. Lassiter," Rhett exclaimed, "We ain't never gonna' bother Yall again. I swear. I'll see to it. I promise. Now let's get help, Dad."

Ron grabbed the reins to Glen's horse. "Damn fool." He said and they rode off.

"That was fast cowboy!" Dad said to Matt

"Just got lucky Mr. Charlie, just lucky I reckon."

"How'd he know you?" Charlie asked.

"I guess he thought I was someone else." Matt replied. "Just mistaken identity, most sure I guess." And Matt walked over to his horse. I swear that was quick, I mean fast! Again I thought of what Mark at the saloon said. If he is Chuck Shoemaker, glad at least he's on our side.

Chapter Eleven

In a couple of days we were just on the North West side of Malvern Arkansas heading toward Little Rock. We ran into some drifters that asked if we needed any help. From the looks of them we didn't need help that bad, at least from the likes of them. They were a rough looking mix. We bid them good day but they fell in behind the herd and followed us. Arnie rode back and asked them why they were following us, and they told him they were heading in the same direction as we were and decided to follow us for safety concerns as this was open rough country. We can't stop anyone from traveling where they want to go, but Arnie didn't like it any. They were a shifty looking bunch and Arnie didn't trust them. He told John Butler to lag back to keep an eye on them. No telling what they had in mind or what they were up to. Amber was at the tail of the herd on the west side and one of the drifters had ridden up next her and was talking to her for quite some time. He finally drifted back with his group and they were laughing about something among themselves. They eased back some and lagged on behind us keeping to themselves. It was getting close to sunset and Cookie had set up to prepare our evening meal. It was a nice location with plenty of grassland for the cattle and a large pond near by. The air was cool and that felt good for a change. I rolled a smoke and sat down and poured me a shot of Cookies shine and waited for the coffee to finish. Cookie had made a stew from a hog he shot with a good amount of potatoes and sourdough bread to soak up the juices. He was testing it occasionally for doneness. It sure smelled good, he knew his stuff. Finally Cookie rang the bell and men lined up, plates in hand to be served. Amber came up and I motioned her to step in front of me.

"I'm OK," she said trying to sound as manly as she could, "You were here first. It sure smells and looks tasty."

"What did that drifter talk to you about?" I quizzed.

"He asked how old I was and how long I've been driving cattle. Where I came from and all sorts of questions like that. He also asked where we going. I told him I wasn't sure and for him to ask the Trail Boss. He gave me the creeps. He kept staring at my chest."

"I don't trust them much," I replied, "I think we should keep an eye on them. That's for sure. I'll feel a lot better when they move on."

"Me too!" Amber said.

We got our meals and she went over and sat with Josh and I went over to Steve and my Dad and sat with them. We talked about our progress, how the cattle were doing, the raids and our good luck so far. We all agreed on the hope for things to go well as we push forward. As long as we got A K out ahead of us on lookout all should go smooth. A K is a good man, we are lucky to have him. As we finished it got dark and I saw a fire where the drifters had set up camp just south of us. I watched Amber with a towel and some fresh clothes going to the pond to get washed up with Josh following behind her to cover her privacy.

I went over to Cookie John and we talked a bit, just small talk. I told him the meal was good and filling.

"That's the way we want it Brad," he said, "Gotta' keep them bellies full. A hungry drover is not a happy one. Wanta' have some more bread?"

"Thanks John, I'm full but if you don't mind I'll take a piece or two for my two horses, if it's OK with you." He smiled and told me to get some and went about cleaning up. I walked over to the corral Carlon had set up and gave the bread to Babe and the Welsh, which I named Prince, because he came from England. They enjoyed their snack and of course begged for more. Then suddenly, as I was rubbing their noses, I heard a scream from over by the pond. I ran in the direction it came from and I saw a man flying through the air! He must have went twenty feet and landed with a thump, face first into the dirt. As I got closer Josh was holding a towel, trying to look away, as he gave it to Amber so she could cover herself. First time I ever saw a black man turn red. Out of respect, I looked away and glad I did as the man Josh had thrown was up on one knee and reached for his pistol. Just as he pulled it out to shoot Josh in the back I pulled my pistol and shot him in the side of the chest and it knocked him over. He quivered a couple of seconds or so and went lifeless.

"Oh my God," Amber yelled, she was trembling, "Thank you Brad, thank you so much."

"He was going to shoot Josh in the back!" I said. "I had to stop him."

"Oh thank you so much, and thank you Josh for getting him off of me. He was all over me." Amber said.

"Glad I could help you Miss Amber," Josh replied, "Thank you Mr. Brad for covering me. He would have shot me if you weren't here."

It didn't take any time at all for almost anyone near to show up to see what had happened. Some of the men knew Andy was a woman and for the one's that didn't there was no doubt now as she stood there with that towel around her and her hair down. There was a lot of buzzing among them and some with a look of shock. Then a couple of the drifters came running up to see for themselves what happened and saw their man on the ground. One went to him and rolled him over.

"Who shot this man?" He hollered. "Who's the man that shot him and why?"

"I did," I answered, "He was trying to molest the lady and then was going to shoot the man that saved her in the back."

"You get your mans body out of here and head for the hills." My Dad shouted. "And I better not see hide nor hair of Yall again. Now get." One of the men acted like he was going to pull his pistol and he suddenly had about eight pointed at him. He decided not to be stupid and helped the other man with the body.

"Arnie, Witt, and John Butler, I want you to follow them and make sure they break camp and pull out." Dad ordered. "Good shootin' Son," He said to me.

"I did what I had to do Dad." I replied. "I can't stand a back stabber or shooter."

I asked the men to back off so Amber could get dressed. She quickly got her clothes on and came and gave me a tight hug.

"Thank you again Brad." She said, and walked back to camp with Josh.

"Well your little secret's out now Son." Dad chuckled with a grin.

"Yea Dad, it sure is. Sorry to keep that from you but we needed the men."

"Son, I wasn't born yesterday. A lot of us knew by day four."

"Who told you Dad?'

"Nobody, it was just her actions. When a man has to relieve himself he just stands next to a tree or bush and lets go. Your feller had to go hide in some bushes. And your feller had narrow shoulders and a strange chest. I mean a little lumpy!" Dad chuckled.

I turned a little red. I was thinking we were getting away with it. But I should have known. Dad's no dummy. I was the dummy thinking I was going to pull this over on him.

"You didn't say anything Dad. Why?"

"Brad we kept an eye on her and we could see she knew what she was doing. This ain't her first drive. Besides, Mike Latimer recognized her, said she was Ben Houston's daughter and he knew Josh also from the Houston Ranch. I never had much dealing with Ben Huston, only met him a time or two in town, and didn't know any of his family. We figured if she couldn't cut it she'd bug out. Surprised us, she did, and she's welcome to drive with us anytime, anywhere. She's a good a cow poke as most of these men here."

"Glad your not mad Dad. I should have known you'd figure it out. Let's go eat."

He put his arm around my shoulder as we walked to the Chuck Wagon. Cookie dished out the fixin's and we dug in. Amber finished quickly and rode out to the herd.

"Guess your glad that's over," John said as I washed my plate.

"Did you know too?" I asked.

"Yup, I've run the Chuck Wagon quite a few times for the Houston outfit. Knew her as soon as I saw her and she knew me too. I told her not to worry, I'd say nothing."

I was glad it's out in the open. Also glad Dad approved of her capabilities. I rolled me a smoke and when finished smoking I hit the blanket. There was a chill in the air. Maybe some rain is coming.

Chapter Twelve

Matt Yeaton woke me up to take his place with the herd and it was starting to rain a light drizzle. I grabbed my slicker and saddled prince and went to the herd. The cattle were grazing but seemed a little restless like they knew something's a brewing. The rain started to come down heavier by the minute. This was going to be miserable. And the cattle were really getting restless and the wind picked up. Suddenly there was a blinding flash and a deafening boom. That's all it took. The cattle rushed in all directions helter skelter, Stampede...... A stampede is bad enough at anytime but in a thunder storm in the dark with driving rain is the worst of all. The constant bolts of lighting and thunder made it hard to contain the cattle and they ran full bore in all directions. You have got to get in front of the leaders and try to turn them. But if your horse stumbles you will most likely be trampled to death. The men in camp all came out as fast as they could to help contain the herd. Not only was I concerned for my safety but for them also. And Amber, where was she? Prince was not a big horse but he had spirit and could run with the best. I got around in the front of the leader steers and was starting to turn them when I saw Amber coming around from the other side. She saw me and spun her steed in my direction to help me contain the running cattle. Suddenly her horse lost its footing and went down. Somehow she managed to land standing with cattle on both sides of her and her horse bolted away leaving her standing next to a scrub oak offering little or no protection. I charged Prince in her direction and grabbed her by the waist. Damn near took me off my horse when I latched on to her. I hung on and Amber grabbed the saddle horn and I cut left out of the running herd. There was a pile of large boulders near by and I dropped her off there for protection. I got back to working the herd. After almost an hour the thunder and lightning finally ceased and the rain was slowing. It took about an hour more before we got things under control and was getting the steers in a group. But we had strays to round up and that would be best done in daylight. I found Amber's horse and went back to get her setting on top of the rock pile. I dismounted and walked the horses to her. She climbed down the rocks and ran over and gave me a hug for dear life.

She looked up and our eyes seemed to lock like she looked into my soul. She was a very lovely lady and I felt a feeling of warmth I haven't felt in a long time.

"Thank you so much Brad. You, you saved my life." She said softly. And we stared at each other for quite a while.

"Glad I was there," I whispered, "You were in trouble lady. I'm just so glad I was there."

"Me too Brad. I feel very lucky." She hugged me again and as she went for her horse and she stopped a second and looked back at me. I think I was blushing. I know I wasn't chilled anymore! I spent the rest of the next day thinking about her as we rounded up strays in every direction. I couldn't get her off my mind.

"We got about three hundred to account for." Arnie said. "Gonna' take today and a good part of tomorrow to round up the rest."

"Ya, they are scattered from here to hell and back." I answered. We spent all day wondering in and out of the brush following tracks picking up four or five here and there in the thick brush and sparse wooded areas. If there are any Indians in these parts, and I'm sure there is, they will be looking also as there are no buffalo of any count to hunt anymore and the steers would be very welcome fare if they can get off with any. The next day after we were finishing breakfast A K came riding in.

"Them drifters got about twenty steers with our brand on them about a mile west." He proclaimed.

"Steve, take five or six men and go with A K," Dad said, "And get them cattle back here. And be careful, get the jump on 'em." My brother Steve gathered up some men and rode off with A K. They caught up with the drifters in about an hour and when they saw our men they abandoned the cattle and high tailed it. Luckily there was no shootin'.

We continued looking for strays, and by noon the next day we had a good head count. We only lost about fifteen steers but Dad said we would pick up some strays from other herds that have been lost from older drives or wild cattle born on the open plains. We have gotten about ten already since we started the drive with no brands on them.

As we were winding up on the next day to stop for camp we got another surprise. Cookies wagons were parked and the fire was burning for the evening meal and there were four bodies laying about thirty yards from John's wagons. Dad and I rode up and Cookie stuck his head out from under the wagon cover.

"What happened?" Dad asked as we dismounted.

"I saw 'em comin'," Cookie said, "So I got in my wagon and got behind my cast iron pots and pans and their bullets just flattened out. They couldn't hit me behind all that armor. They kept' a shootin' and the pots kept' a ringing and when they got about thirty yards or so, I stuck my Spencer slam gun out and hit 'em with buckshot. Boy was they surprised as I blew 'em off their horses." It was the drifters. Cookie got them all so we wont be having problems from them any longer.

"We got six more horses and gear to add to our stock." Dad said.

"Wanta scalp 'em?" A K asked John.

"Na, you can have 'em"

"I dint kill 'em." A K answered. "Don't want no scalp I
dint earn. No self respecting Injun especially a Sioux would
do that"

Dad just shook his head. "Good thing you got in that
wagon with all that iron John." He said. "Sure saved your
hide."

"Ya, it put me behind a little, but I'll get dinner going here
quickly." John answered.

"Need any help, Cookie?" Amber offered.

"If ya like dear, I could use an extra hand, sure would be
appreciated." They went on to make 'in dinner; she looked
at me often with a warm smile. She sure was a lovely Lady.

We went on and buried the bodies of the drifters. We
found no identification on any of the men so that's all we
could do. We even said a prayer over them. At least we
were respectful. We sat down to eat dinner; Amber sat with
Josh but kept looking over at me. I smiled at her and she
would smile back. It gave me a warm feeling, but I thought
of Judy at times and it mad me feel a little odd. I did love
her so much but this lady was getting a lot of my attention.
Making me feel guilty. How was Judy feeling up there
looking down on this? Is it wrong to feel like I was? It'll
wear off I thought. I'm sure it will. I think it will! Of course
it will. Wont it?

We pushed on and it was hot and humid. It was taking a
toll on all of us including the cattle and the horses. We

were making good time but we didn't want to push the stock too hard or fast. In a couple of days we were west of Little Rock and starting to cross the Arkansas River. The water was not too deep, deep enough but the current was not bad at all and we got the men and the herd across safely. The cattle, horses and our men got some most needed water.

On the other side it was rock and brush with scattered trees. You sure could see where we had been as the herd flattened a lot of brush and broke some of the small trees. Every once and a while, we could see a warrior or two on the mesas watching our movements. As long as they stayed there that would be fine. A K said they looked like Kiowa and he said they might try to grab a stray and if they did they wouldn't try to stampede the herd. We were picking up a stay steer here and there so the loss of one or two of our herd wouldn't hurt us. Most likely the Kiowa would end up with a stray themselves and think it was ours.

Amber would ride up occasionally and ask how I was doing and making small talk. I liked the look of her long Auburn hair blowing in the breeze. It looked like red-gold. The ground was getting rockier and there was more brush then prairie grass which made it hard pickings for the stock. And of course it slowed us down some but we had to push on. A K really laid out a good trail for us. So far we only ran into one fenced area and Dad made a deal with the rancher and he let us drive through. That was good because it saved us several miles if we had to go around. We were coming up on the west side of the town of Cabot. That put us about half way across Arkansas making very good time as it's the middle of July and we are twenty three days into the drive. The only thing slowing us down now was the land had a steady up grade and we getting to a higher elevation. More rock and less trees but good grass all along. Water would be scarce except for small ponds here and there as there had been some rain in the area for a couple of days. We wouldn't see any big water until we started down hill again.

Chapter Thirteen

Back in Texas at the Berman Ranch Glen and Rhett were resting and taking care of their wounds, not much had been said of the blunders' and loss of men they experienced over the foiled ambush attempts on the Lassiter herd. Ron Hargrove and his men were staying in the bunkhouse with who was left of the Berman's hands. Rhett had his arm in a sling and his Dad's shoulder was still bandaged and sore but both should recover just fine. Rhett got some coffee and asked his Dad if he wanted any. He declined. Rhett sipped his coffee looking out the window and turned to his Dad.

"Father, I am going into Lufkin and ask Sherriff Royal to accompany me to the Lassiter ranch so I don't get shot at."

"What for son?" Glen asked, with a puzzled look on his face.

"I am going to see Mrs. Lassiter and offer her any help she might need doing."

"The hell you are, we got a' nuff work here if your bent on doing things."

"Dad it's about time we settled down and made our selves worthy of the community. I am tired of our dirty work and shady dealings. We have gotten some good men killed and we've killed some good men and it's time we stopped. I don't want to be looking over my shoulder all the time for a lawman or some hired gun." Glen sat there with a bewildered look on his face.

"This is my own son telling me this? We are settling son," Glen spoke in a treating tone. "We got this ranch and we are staying here and building up our herd."

"Yes Dad," Rhett answered, "And just how did we get this ranch, and most of the cattle Dad? We stole them all! We ain't doin' it no more. I'm tired of it"

"You sit your butt down and cool off, son." Glen said to Rhett.

"I'm cool enough to do what has to be done, Dad, and we are going to start by helping the Lassiter's! If you don't agree to go straight I'm gonna tell everyone how you had the Houston ranch torched so we could take it over."

"Like hell you are, if you step out this door I swear I'll shoot ya." Glen threatened.

"Dad, you gonna' shoot me in the back, your own son? I don't think so." Rhett turned and started out the door. Glen Berman grabbed his pistol and pointed it at Rhett. Then swore to blue heaven and threw it across the room and grabbed his shoulder in pain. Then he kicked every chair in the room. He was really angry.

Rhett had one of the hands help him saddle up and rode off to Lufkin.

When he got to Lufkin he met up with Sheriff George Royal explained what he had to do and asked if he would ride to the Lassiter ranch with him so there would be no trouble. The Sheriff agreed it would be a good idea and told him about the warning telegram he received. They mounted up and rode out to see Mrs. Lassiter.

 Ron Hargrove and his men rode into Lufkin and hitched their horses at the rail in front of Jeanne's Saloon. They walked to the Sheriff's office and deposited their pistols with the deputy in charge and returned to the Saloon. Mark Foor remembered Ron from years ago and greeted him.

"Howdy Ron," Mark said, "How ya been doing. Long time no see."

"Good to see ya Mark. How long you been here?"

"About a year, got tired of Nevada, too much shootin'. And speak' in of shootin' I here Glen Berman got shot and his son too!"

"Yea, damn fool tried to pull on Chuck Shoemaker." Ron told him. "Big mistake."

"Chuck Shoemaker? Where did you run into him?" Mark asked.

"He's riding with the Lassiter drive. I recognized him right away and tried to warn 'em but Glen wouldn't listen to me. That man is lighting fast. He ain't slowed down none a' tall. That's one deadly hand with a pistol. Glen only got his hand on his grip, never got ta pull it out of the holster. Could' a killed him but he chose not too!"

"I saw him in here when he signed up for the drive but he said his name was Matt Barnes." Mark replied. "So I thought maybe I was mistaken but he sure looked like Chuck and I asked Brad about him. He said he signed as Matt Barnes and maybe he just looked like him. But I wasn't so sure. I never forget a face. Do the Lassiter's know now who he is?"

"Don't know as we didn't have a friendly talk to talk meeting. I just wanted out' a there, and no more trouble"

"What ya doing now? Hangin' a round or moving out?" Mark asked.

"Me and the boy's might stay a while and help Glen with his cattle. They are scattered everywhere right now. Just have 'ta see how it goes." Ron and his men had a drink or two at the bar and moved to a table. Kim the waitress asked if they wanted lunch and some coffee. Most had coffee and a few ordered some sandwiches.

Rhett met with Becky Lassiter and she was impressed with the young man's actions and she figured his mom must have had some influence on his up-bringing as he was very formal and polite. She thanked him for his offer of help and told him he was welcome to come by anytime. She served some coffee and cookies and the three of them chatted for quite a while. Rhett thanked her and Sherriff Royal; he then excused himself and rode back to his home.

Ron Hargrove and his men drank coffee and ate a little. Kim Johnson came to the table.

"You boy's staying the night? If you are we have some pretty ladies that would love to keep ya' comfy."

"No," Ron relied, "We're gonna' play a little cards and head back the ranch."

"It's a shame!" Kim answered. "You're missing out of spending time with some sweeties."

"Thanks anyway, dear but we don't have the time. Do we boy's."

"I might stay." One of them said. "See me later." She gave him s thumbs up and went to the bar.

A slicker in a Tweed suit sitting at a card table said to Ron, "Wanta' play a few friendly rounds?" "I play for money." Ron said "Well sit on down and lets play," the slicker pointed to a seat, "Let's have some fun"

Ron and one of his men, LaDon Drawdy, took a seat and each bought twenty dollars of chips. They played for an hour or so and the pot went back and forth slowly built up to a couple hundred dollars in Ron's favor and He called the slicker as he threw down another twenty dollars. The slicker threw down his hand. "Read 'em and weep," he said, "three aces and two jacks." Ron looked at the cards with anger in his face.

"You cheat 'in buzzard." He said angrily and threw his cards down. "Two aces, and three Queens."

"When did a deck get five aces," Ron demanded, "you playing me for a fool? I'll take that pot and then I'm gonna' whip your hide. I can't stand a cheat." Ron stood up and raked the money on the table toward him. The slicker stood up with a derringer in his hand and hollered, "No ya don't cowhand that's mine." Ron grabbed the table and threw it into him, chips and money going everywhere. He then stepped on the slickers hand and kicked the gun away. He then grabbed the cheat by his collar and proceeded to punch him senseless and threw him against the bar. "Help me pick up my money and let's get out 'a here." Ron said to LaDon, they gathered the money and left.

Chapter Fourteen

We continued to the top of the high ground and it leveled off for a stretch. The cattle were tired and so were we. It was a long up hill journey. Our horses were tired also but that Cracker horse that Mr. Witt rode never seems to slow down. He acts as fresh at the end of the day as when he started. Also that Welsh horse Prince I switch with, even though he's a little smaller that the other horses, he never seems to wear down either. He has spirit. We had lost a few cattle in the stampede, but so far we have picked up about two hundred wild and stray cattle on our drive. That is a real bonus. The air was a little cooler at this height and most of the water from the rain had dried up or sunk into the ground faster than we thought it would. We ran into small pools here and there and it didn't take long for the cattle to drink them dry and turn them into a mud wash...

"Let's give 'em a break!" Arnie the trail boss shouted. That was good to hear, we needed a rest. We let the herd spread out some to graze. Some did and others simply laid down with their noses to the ground, they were tired after that long up hill grind. A K came riding in and told us to be alert as he saw several Warriors today. "I gotta' uneasy felling that they are looking for trouble." He warned. We didn't need any trouble I said to my Dad and he agreed.

"We'll split into two shifts and put sentries around the herd, keep a look out." Dad ordered. The only fair way to do it was draw cards from a hat. Dad put an even number of face cards and number cards in the hat and had the men draw. All that got a face card went first. I got lucky and got a five.

The men got a quick bite to eat and mounted up and rode out to the cattle. Amber got a nine so she got to stay in camp also. I rolled a smoke and sat on a box near the fire and she came and joined me. We talked about the heat, the rain and how far we've came.

Cookie walked to us with a bottle in his hand.

"Want a drink?" He asked.

"Sure John, I'll take a nip." I poured some into my cup.

"Want some Amber?" I asked.

"Sure I'll try a little, Brad, thanks." I poured a little into her cup and she took a sip. That opened her eyes. "Wow," she said, "that's got a kick to it." It was probably close to a hundred proof. She poured a little water to blend it down.

"Spoiling good drink." Cookie said with a grin and walked off.

We did some small talk and Amber asked. "Do you think those braves A K saw will cause trouble?"

"I don't know, but I think it will be after darkness is upon us if they are Sioux or Comanche. Apaches' don't like fighting at night." I replied. "I hope not though, as we and the herd needs rest." She looked toward the herd.

"Yes they do for sure, Brad, and we are tired too." We ate a good meal of deer Cookie shot and potato's with biscuits', we washed our plates and laid back and took a nap. I was thinking about those Indians, and their intentions worried me a little. In the older times Indians didn't take much to fighting at night but as more white men came and things got tougher they changed their strategies, and night raids became more common, all but the Apaches. The last year of my hitch in the cavalry we got several attacks at night and that makes for tough fight 'in. My buddy Jeff Cushing woke me up for my shift and I shook Amber to wake her. We saddled up and went to be with the herd. It was quiet, too much so. Most nights you could hear coyotes and wolves howling or a puma scream, but not tonight. That meant that there were things moving around they didn't like and that made then spooky. As luck would have it we got though the night unchallenged and all was safe. We rode in for breakfast and washed our hands and faces. Cookie handed out bowls this morning instead of plates. That's odd.

"What's this, tastes awful crunchy?" One of the men asked. "Oatmeal," Cookie answered. "Shut up and eat." I looked at mine. "Oatmeal, where did you get that, John?"

"Had a couple of bags of oat's I'd brought along for my mules but the second bag got mites in it, so I couldn't feed it to my mules. Might make 'em sick. So I ground it up, and maked' oatmeal."

"Holly cow Cookie, with mites in it?" Arnie said. "Shut up and eat, there cooked ain't they, won't hurt ya, adds a little spice to it. Might make bread out 'a it too!" John blurted back.

"Don't taste too bad really." Matt Yeaton said. "Gotta little sugar, Cookie?"

"All right, move 'em out boys," Arnie shouted, "let's get 'em' moving, times a wasting." We saddled up and started moving the herd. There was a breeze in our faces and I could tell the cattle could smell water as they picked up pace. Almost to fast. We were now a little north west of the town of Searcy according to my map I carried. We had to get out front and try to slow the herd. The smell of water in their noses was strong and they wanted to get to it. In fact we all needed to fill up and Cookie needed to fill his barrels too! We moved on and the pace quickened even with us trying to slow them down. It went from a trot to almost a down right run by afternoon. It was hard to slow them as the water must have been close. We went over a rise and a small river, about a hundred yards wide, was in front of us about a quarter mile ahead.

"Get out the way and let them go." Arnie hollered, and the whole herd charged for the stream. It was about three feet deep and they waded in and drank and splashed and rolled like a bunch of kid's on a picnic. It was clear and cold. Some of the men hung their pistols on their saddle and jumped in, felt good!

"Let's hold 'em here." Dad said. We'll make camp here, water up and we all can get some rest." That sounded good. We had to go up stream to get clear water as the herd had it churned up real good. Amber went further up with Josh behind her so she could get a bath. Cookie John got there before we did and figured it would be a good stopping place also. He had got his barrels filled and set up camp for the evening meal. I washed up as best I could, rolled a smoke and sat down with the men around the fire and got some coffee. Amber and Josh came back and joined up with us. Josh went to see my Dad.

"Mister Lassiter, Sir," he said, "I wanta tell you I saw a lot of Injun pony tracks up the stream where Missy Amber washed up. Lots 'a tracks Sir."

"Thank ya Josh," Dad replied, "A K told me he saw 'em too! We need to be on top of our game." Dad ordered. "Yall need to keep your rifles close an ready tonight. We can't take no chances. Sooner or later they will make a move on us. You can bet on that!"

We bunked down after talking around the fire for a while.
We needed a rest. It was a little nippy this evening, the
coldest we have had so far. Cookie got the fire going
nicely, it felt so good. Even Amber came out from under
John's wagon and slept near me. My brother Steve and A K
took their rifles and blankets and left camp. I hoped they
would be warm enough.

 After eating breakfast we started off heading north east
skirting east of Heber Springs. I told Dad when we got
close to the next town I would ride in and telegram Mom
and tell her we were doing well. He thought that would be a
good Idea. He said the next town was Batesville and we
would be skirting close to it. Amber rode up.

"Chilly last night," she said, "I almost got up against you
for warmth, but thought better of it." I looked at her with a
smile. "That would have been fine by me as I was a tad
light on blanket. Wouldn't chased ya off." She smiled
blushingly and rode forward up the herd.

 About ten in the morning we saw two riders coming up
behind us. They didn't look menacing, just riding casually.
From the dust on them they have been riding with out
stopping for a while. They rode up to Don Volsch and
Howard Branden and asked, "Where's the boss man?" Don
Volsch pointed to my Dad. "See that man up there on the
big grey? That's him, names Charlie, Charlie Lassiter."
They thanked him and trotted on to my Dad.

"Howdy Boss Man, gotta' minute?"

"What ya need boys?" Dad questioned.

Want 'a know if you'd be need 'in a couple of gun hands? You're going through some pretty rough country, Injuns, rustlers and all, might need some support."

"Well boys I'm on a tight budget," Dad told them, "Can't afford it, a tall. Be nice, but can't see how I can do it. Just things all spoken for money wise"

"Well the way I look at it, Boss" one said, "Where you're about to go you can't not afford it, and the price is right! Just feed us. We ain't ask 'in for money, just feed us and we'll ride with ya four 'ta five days. We know a little bout driving steers too!" Charlie looked at them closely. They didn't look all that dangerous and probably would look better when cleaned up. He thought if we keep a close eye on them to make sure they didn't steal anything it would be good to have an extra gun or two with Indian trouble most likely coming up.

"O K boys, ya gotta' deal. What's you names?"

"Call me Robert and that's Harry." One answered.

"See ya for the even 'in meal boys!" Dad told them and rode forward. The two men split up and helped driving the herd. Where we were now you could see where cattle had been moved on this trail by the thousands years ago. They laid out a trail that had ground the vegetation and top soil to bed rock two hundred yards wide. Just some sparse scrub brush here and there. The land had been laid to almost nothing but barren ground. It had rained earlier so the dust was not a factor. You could tell we had gained elevation as the temperature was dropping. Cool to chilly nights and mornings. The heat in the day was not so bad either, mid eighties, and that made the drive more tolerable. We kept the herd moving at a good pace and it seemed no time at all we caught up to Cookie John for our mid day nooner. He had the coffee going and a big pot of thick soup was cooking with fresh bread. I dismounted and tied my horse to one of his wagon wheels and poured myself some coffee.

"We be gettin' close to Batesville soon," John said, "I'll be need 'en some supplies. Tell yer Dad fer me!"

"Sure will Cookie, Dad wants me to send a telly to Mom also and let her know how we are doing and check on her welfare too!" I told him. "I'll get a man and about six pack horses. I'd better check with the men for there needs also."

"Good idea, Brad they gonna need some smoke fixins' for sure I bet."

"Yeah John, I'm getting low my self." As I was finishing my soup I noticed Matt Barnes talking with the new guys, Robert and Harry. They were joking and laughing like three ole guys talking over old stories. Arnie hollered to move 'em out and we got mounted and started the cattle rolling. Amber waved at me and went to the far side of the herd. I got with my Dad and told him of John needing supplies and he said also we were not far from Batesville and we should get what we needed there. He was planning on Walnut Ridge as it was a bigger town, but it shouldn't matter much.

Chapter Fifteen

We drove until about five in the afternoon and came to a vast area with lots of grass, a lake for water and Cookie had set up. So Trail Boss Arnie bellowed, "Hold 'em up," with his hat held high and waving, "hold 'em here boy's." A few men ran to the front of the herd to stop them but the cattle seemed to know before we did as they were eating grass and wading in the lake already.

A K came riding in and told Dad and Arnie he saw several warriors traveling in small bands today but they seemed to be moving north east ahead of our group, not paying us any mind. He said they appeared to be Sioux and Comanche's. He also noted they had no war paint on but that could change any day. Another thing he was looking for and couldn't find was their camp sites, where the Squaws and children were. He didn't find any so he figured most likely they were not from this area and that wasn't such good news either. Dad sent the word out to the men and told them to keep a sharp eye out for trouble. Sooner or later we may have all we want.

Cookie John had a small elk he had shot earlier in the day on a spit over the fire with potato's and a green that he picked some where that he called wild spinach. I've had elk cooked by him before, and I knew it would be good. He rang the dinner bell.

"Get your knives out and cut off what ya want. Help your selves." He ordered as he handed out the plates. Amber came in line and I motioned her to go ahead of me.

"Thank you Brad," she said as she curtsied blushingly, "Looks real good. I never had elk like this before."

"It tastes just like beef," I replied, "I like mine on the rare side. Do you want me to carve some for you?" She held out her plate.

"Please do, I would like that, Brad, thank you for being so helpful." She had washed and combed her hair and had a rosy tint to her cheeks. Sorta' had all the men's attention. Robert, one of the strangers asked if she wanted to sit next to him. "Oh thank you but I am sitting with Josh and Mr. Brad. But thank you for asking" She pulled up a box and sat next to me. "Where did they come from, Brad? Do you know them?"

"No I don't but Dad told them they could ride with us. The extra guns could be a big help if they know how to used 'em. And Dad said they only wanted meals for pay, so that's a good deal I think."

"They seem to know our man Matt." She answered. "They spend a lot of time riding together."

"I noticed that also, Amber, they act like some old cronies going over past times to me. Maybe they've met somewhere before. Maybe met driftin' or herding cattle, or had a drink together in a saloon sometime back. Who knows? They seem like nice enough men, well mannered too. They work well with the cattle also. One thing, if we have trouble extra pistols and rifles is good insurance."

"One of them rode near me for a while today," Amber told me, "he seemed nice enough. And as you said, very polite and well mannered." We and the men ate all the elk we could, it was really good, and I was stuffed.

"Come on y'all," John said, "eat up. Don't get no better than that here boys." But the men had enough and then some. They all raved about how good it was and thanked Cookie for such a fine meal. Amber and Josh helped John with the clean up as he cut what was left of the Elk off the bones and put it a small barrel with some brine on top to keep it from spoiling. Amber and I sipped some coffee and chatted for a while. I rolled a smoke and looked into her eyes. She is a lovely lady, such fine features, smooth skin, and a glint in her eyes. It makes me feel guilty though, as thoughts of Judy keep coming into my mind. She was a lovely and warm lady too! But when I look into Amber's eyes I get this feeling like she was drawing me in. Her beauty and manners are working on me deeply. But should I even think and feel this way? I don't really know. I feel guilty.

I was getting ready to rollup and Mike Latimer walked up to me.

"Hi Mike, doing OK?"

"Yea, you didn't say anything," Mike answered, "so I figured you didn't see it or didn't care."

"See what Mike?"

"There's a Buff in the herd. Saw him this morn. He's near the front and just trodden along like he's part of the bunch. Ain't cause 'in no trouble, just movin' with the cattle he is."

"Don't see many Buffs now days Mike. Most of 'em been wiped out! Damn few left, it's a shame there were millions at one time. As long as he isn't making trouble let him go. He'll most likely leave some where along the way. But don't get in front of him, they anger easy"

"That's what I figured, Brad. Maybe he's just lookin' for a lady friend. You have a good sleep."

"Thanks Mike, see ya in the morning." I rolled into my blanket. The air was chilly and damp tonight. Maybe more rain coming our way. I just hope it's not a thunder storm. I've seen a couple of tornados in the distance but luckily they were not near, thank heavens. My Dad told me of one that hit a cattle drive years ago and he said it made a real mess. Loss of men and a large loss of cattle. He said some of the men were never found. I fell asleep quickly but was awakened by someone snuggling up to me. It felt nice and warm shortly, hope its Amber and not one of the men or a mountain lion. Maybe the Buff? I went back to sleep, after all warm is good no matter the source.

I woke in the morn before daybreak. Who ever it was had gone but left an extra blanket on me. That was nice because it was real chilly this morning. I laid there for a minute and gathered my thoughts then got up and walked around Cookies wagon and checked his wheels so to speak and when I walked back around. Amber was standing there with a grin on her face. She held out a cup.

"Coffee Brad?" She asked.

"Thanks, I can sure use one. I was warm last night Miss Amber, and you?"

"I knew it was going to be colder and there was no room around the fire with all the men around it so I threw my blanket over you and cuddled up. When you started snoring I got your blanket and mine over both of us. Hope you didn't mind"

"No I didn't but anyone of the men including me would have moved if you had asked."

"I didn't want to impose on anyone's feelings or take advantage just because I'm a woman. I told you when I signed up I'm just one of the men and that's how I want to be treated. I've made several drives with my Dad and I know what it's like to be cold. No pleasure at all. Besides snuggling up to you I felt protected, knowing how light a sleeper you are." Her face was alive and so much color in her cheeks.

"Glad you felt safe and comfortable. You sure kept me warm, I thank you." Little did she know that I was so comfy that the Buffalo in the herd could have trampled me and I wouldn't have cared, let alone woke up? She looked so lovely this morn for some reason and her eyes were warm and looking right into me. I really don't know what to do. She is getting to my feelings and I feel so strange, what would Judy think? We finished eating and saddled up. Amber and Josh rode to the far side of the herd. The trail boss, Arnie, bellowed, "RO-L-L-L-L 'EM out boy's, times a wastin." Mr. Witt cracked his whip a couple of times and other just hooped and hollered. The cattle started moving.

The air was warming up quickly but the dust was not a problem as the ground was damp. The Buff had moved up further to the front of the herd and was moving well with the cattle causing no problems. It sure was a strangest sight that I or the rest of the men had never seen or heard of ever taking place before. But he acted like he belonged. Maybe he was just lonely. On the drive so far I only noticed four or five Buffs in the distance. Not many of them left now days. Hard to imagine, as there were thousands of them twenty years ago.

As I was riding and pushing cattle I kept thinking about Amber snuggling up to me last night. Just couldn't get it off my mind. She sure was a looker and soft to be near. On the job she was as good as anyone of the men. But in camp her lady side was showing so more open. She had the attention of the men, that's for sure. I hoped there would not be any trouble come of it but we had good men. In the west men admired women and didn't take to anyone roughing a lady up no matter her looks and treated them with respect. It was the outlaws, drifters and rustler's that would take a chance on violating a lady and none of our men would be a worry unless maybe a drink or more too many could cause a poor choice of judgment.

Dad came riding up next to me.

"How's it going Son?" He asked. "Doing O K?"

"Yes Dad, but I gotta' talk to you a minute or two if you don't mind."

He gave me a worried look and asked.

"Something troubling you Son? Or is it something about the herd going on that's bothering you?"

I started telling him about Amber and how she was on my mind and my guilty feelings about thinking that way. I told him I was attracted to her but wasn't sure if it was right to feel that way. He looked at me with a stern look of wisdom in his eyes that he's had ever since I can remember from the time I was a young 'in when he had something to say of importance.

"Son, I can understand how you feel, and your guilt of what Judy may think of you. But she's gone Son, and that ain't gonna' change no matter what you do. You can decide to be a loner and be miserable for the rest of your life or you can latch on to a lady such as Amber and live a happy productive life. And the way I see it, when you go to the Great Plains above, the good Lord will get things straightened out. Sure, Judy is watching but she wants you to be happy and not pine away over her. Your short life together was very loving and warm but she can't help you now. She would want you to carry on."

I thought of what my dad said to me and it made me feel so much better. Dad was right, as usual. He always had a good mind for thinking and straightening things out.

"Thanks dad," I said, "I appreciate your advice and you taking the time to listen."

"That's what dads do Son. I am always ready to listen when you or any of the men have a problem. I try to have the right answer, but mostly I say what I feel is the truth as best as I can."

"Thanks Dad, you have always showed me the right trail." I answered.

"By the way son. We are nearing Batesville so in about a hour why don't you take a man and hook a team to John's small wagon and a couple of pack horses to get the supplies he needs and pick up the men's wants'?

"O K Dad, I'll get it taken care off and get right back."

"I'll meet you at Cookies wagon and give you the money you'll need for the goods. Might just as well stay the night and head back in the morning Brad. No sense being in a big hurry, get some rest and a hot bath."

"That will be nice, dad, but I will make good time getting back in the morning."

"O K Brad, I'll see ya in an hour at John's wagon." He shook my hand and rode off. I started riding around to the men getting a list of what they needed. Most wanted fixin's for smoking, some candy and a few wanted new socks or bandanas. When I got to Amber I told her I was going into town and asked her if she wanted anything.

"I'd like to get some chocolate if they have any." She replied. "It would be nice to mix it with my coffee. Your not going alone are you?"

"No I'm going to get one of the men to ride with me. It'll be good to have an extra eye and gun in this country."

"Can I go with you?" She asked. "Well I'm going to be staying over night." I told her.

"I've got money for a room Brad, and besides, it would be nice to get a hot bath for a change. I'll bring my pistol and my rifle too!" I thought it over for a minute. It would be nice to have her for company. I would have some time to talk and feel things out.

"OK, see ya in an hour at Cookie's wagon." She smiled, and thanked me; her eyes were sparkling with a look of joy.

Chapter Sixteen

I got a list of needs from the men and went over to get
Cookies list of the supplies he needed. Then I went to
Carlon and got two horses to hook up to the wagon and two
more for packing extras if I need too. As I was getting the
team ready Dad came over and gave me the money for the
goods.
"Who ya taking with ya?" He asked.
"Amber is going to ride with me," I told him, "Maybe we
can talk a little and I can sort of see what her mind is
thinking. She can shoot well too, that could be a help if I
need it." He thought for a minute and replied.
"Good, that will give you some time to talk and feel things
out, good decision my boy, get your head cleared."
"That I will do, dad. Gives me time to work out my
feelings some what. I'm also going to take a pair of pack
horses with me just in case."
"That's a good idea Son, you might need them. Hope
Cookie's not going to break me." He said laughingly.
"Take your time and be safe. Here's a map I drew out for
you to get to town. Follow the trail west along the White
River. It goes straight to Batesville. It should be a good trail
as the people use it to go back and forth from there to
Newport. After you get the supplies cross the river and

head north east to the town of Walnut Ridge and you will catch up to us"

"Thanks dad, I'll catch up with you tomorrow." He patted me on the back and told me he was going to ride to the head of the herd as they were getting ready to cross the White River. I got the pack horse from Carlon and Amber came to me and threw her bag in the wagon and climbed into the seat.

"Come on cowboy, times a wasting." Now she sounds like Arnie the trail boss I thought to my self. This is going to be interesting. I got on the seat next to her and we moved out. We chatted a little small talk for a while about the cattle herd, the buffalo, the men we had and the two strangers. The country around us was alive with color. The trees along the trail were so many shades of green and yellows. The sun light on the rocky hills had so many hues of red, orange and yellow. The river was sparkling from the rays of the sun. It sure was pretty country. We didn't talk for a time, just looking at the beauty of the land. After a while I noticed Amber had slid over closer next to me. I wasn't sure what to say about my feelings toward her or how to even start. We just sat there quiet for a while then she put her hand on my thigh and gave me a look of concern.

"Brad, can I ask you how you feel about me?" Well that sure broke the ice for sure but I was tongue tied, I had a million things to say but I froze up.

"Well," she asked, "Cat got your tongue?" I looked her in the eyes and replied.

"I was gonna ask you the same thing and was trying to get up the nerve to do so. I didn't want to seem to bold or forward. I think you are very pretty lady and I really like being around you."

"Brad I like being around you also. You're a good looking man and a fine catch for any lady. That's for sure."

"I don't know about being a good catch but I can protect myself and mine. I have been watching you and you've been watching me it seems. I hope I'm not being to forward."

"Yes I have been watching you, and that night I snuggled to you I felt so warm and alive. Never felt that way before!"

"So did I, and I could get used to that, that's for sure." We looked at each other like two love sick cows.

"Well let's just see where it leads us Brad. You don't really know me well and I am learning about you. But I gotta' tell you, I like what I see Brad." Things got real quiet again between us but my head was spinning away, as I liked what I saw too!

We rode into Batesville and still had a couple of hours of daylight to get around with. It seemed like a nice little town. There were a lot of heavy wagons pulling loads of rock to the rail yard. Batesville became a town because of the rock mines near by and the railroad. It was a bustling little place with about two thousand residents a couple of saloons and several stores. I asked a man where the livery stable was and he told me it was just down the street on the right. We drove to the stable and a short stocky man came over to meet us.

"Howdy folk's can I help ya?" He asked.

"I'd like to put the horses up for the night Sir." I told him. He smiled and said, "Just put 'em up, two bits each. Feed 'em all, another four bits for all."

"That will be just fine, sir, fair enough." I agreed.

"It's not going to rain tonight, I'm pretty sure of that," he answered, "so I'll leave them in the corral. If it rains I'll bring 'em in. I shook his hand and asked what store he would recommend for the supplies I needed. He looked at my lists and looked down the street. He looked at the list again and pointed at a red store front about a hundred yards down the street. "That's Clifton's Whole Goods." He said. "Good honest man and should have all you need and his prices are right. He'll treat ya well. I buy from him myself, he's good to deal with. Tell 'em I sent ya."

I thanked him and he said he would take care of the horses and the wagon. Amber and I took our bags and things and walked down the street to the store. The street was busy. People were going to the saloons and shops to have a drink or get supplies. We went into the Clifton's store; it was very orderly and neatly laid out and quite a few shoppers getting needs. "Hi folks," a young man said to us, "Can I be of any help to find what you need?"

"You must be Mr. Edge," I answered, "I have a list of things I need to take back to camp for my outfit."

"Call me Cliff," he said," No need to be that formal. Let me see what you need." I handed him the list and he looked it over.

"How soon you need these?" He asked.

"When it's convenient for you Mr. Cliff. I know it's a short notice but in the morning would be great."

He smiled, "No problem my friend, I'll have it ready for you to load up behind the store about nine in the morning. If that's O K?"

"That will be fine sir. Can you recommend a good rooming house for us to sleep tonight, and where I can send a telegram?" I asked.

"Just down the street is Leslie Montgomery's hotel." He replied. "She's a nice lady, help you all she can. It's clean and tidy, good meals and has a bath house with hot water. And she doesn't take in any ruffians. Good safe place. This is a good town with no trouble pretty much. Maybe once in a while something might happen at one of the saloons but on a whole, mostly quiet. Good bunch of people here. The post office is just down past her hotel"

I bought a new shirt, a few socks and a couple of undie's. I also bought some ready rolled smokes, never saw those before, convenient though. Amber bought some socks a new pair of denim pants and a long night shirt.

"Thanks Cliff, we will be back in the morning, have a good evening." Amber and I looked around for a couple of minutes more. He had a good supply of just about anything you would need. Nice, clean and well arranged store.

Chapter Seventeen

 Ron Hargrove and LaDon Drawdy were helping Berman's
men round up stray cattle in the heavy brush at the edge of
a Mesa.
"Never seen so many different brands on a ranch in my
life." Ron said with a frown on his face. "Somebody from
around here comes a ridin' out here there just might be a
hangin' or two."
 "He better have bill of sales for these cows," LaDon said,
"Or there could be a lot of questions and somebody better
have some good answers."
 "If he don't have proof of sale for these cows, I don't want
no part of this. We'd better have a talk with Glen bout this.
I don't want my neck stretched for no cow I didn't steal."
Ron answered.
Suddenly a shot was fired and took Ron's hat off. They
pulled their rifles and looked in the area the shot was fired
from but the sun was in their eyes and they couldn't see
anything. "Get down," Ron hollered to LaDon, and they
dismounted and took what cover they could find. Another
shot rang out and it hit LaDon's rifle and the splinters from
the stock cut his arm in a couple places and the blood was
dripping from several small wounds.

"Someone is up on the side of that Mesa," Ron said, "Think it's an Injun? Don't know why anyone else would be a shootin' at us less it's somebody that owns some of these here cows."

"Could be," LaDon answered, "But I'm thinkin' Injun too!"

"You O K?" Ron asked. "It's not as bad as it looks Ron, just a bunch of deep scratches. Could 'a been worse." They ran into some heavy tree cover and tried to figure where the shots were coning from. Ron saw some movement about fifty feet up the Mesa. Then another shot came at them hitting the tree Ron was behind and split bark from it.

"Up by that big dark rock about fifty feet up." LaDon said as he pointed.

'That's where I saw someone move," Ron answered, "Fire a couple of shots at him to cover me. I'm gonna try to flank him." LaDon fired some shots around and to side of the rock and Ron ran hard to the left and took cover about thirty yards over and waited. He saw someone move just enough for him to take a shot. He fired and there was a cry of pain. The man went to move and LaDon took a shot at him and he rolled forward into the open not moving.. "I got him!" LaDon yelled to Ron. "Good," Ron replied, "Let's see who it is." They climbed up the slope and discovered it was a white man. Ron rolled him over and saw it was the card shark that tried to cheat him in Jeanie's saloon. "I'll be damned LaDon," Ron exclaimed, "Did he think he was going to get his money back from us? Or just trying to even the score by killin' us?"

"If he was a better shot he'd a got us, I'll say that pal." LaDon said. "What shall we do with him?"

Ron looked around and said, "Let's find his horse and put him on it. The horse will know where to go." They followed the man's tracks for about a hundred yards and found a gap in the Mesa wall. The horse was tethered to a sapling growing out of the rocks. They took the mare to where the man's body laid. They got him over the saddle and tied him to it. After leading the horse out, they smacked it on the rump and she took off in the direction of town. They went back and mounted their horses and started pushing the cattle they had rounded up back to the pasture near the Berman's house. Rhett came to meet them. "See you boys got some strays."

"Yes we did but a lot of them have different brands." Ron answered. "If yer keeping them we don't want no more parts of working around here. I ain't gonna' get lynched over no cows I didn't have a part in." Rhett looked at the cows and then to Ron.

"I'm going to get the boys to pick out the ones that aren't ours and take 'em back to the ranches they belong to in the morning. Dad will be mad but he's going to go straight if it's the last thing I do!"

"Good for you son," Ron said, "The old days are over and it ain't worth hanging over no cow." Ron and LaDon washed up and they and a couple of the Berman men decided to ride into town for a drink at Jeanie's. When they got to town they dropped their pistols off at the sheriff's office. The mare they tied the man on was hooked to the rail in front of the sheriff's porch. They said nothing opting not to arouse any questions.

Ron and his men went into Jeanie's and it was busy. They made room at the bar.

"Howdy Ron," Mark the bartender greeted them, "Been working hard? What 'cha ya have?"

"I think the men want a shot of whisky," Ron replied, "Been pushing cattle here and there. How's things in town?"

"Been mostly quiet till this afternoon," Mark answered as he poured shots of whisky, "Then that card cheat Barry Moore came riding in draped and tied over his saddle deader than a rabbit in a Puma's mouth. Sherriff Royal's look 'in into it. Who ever shot him at least didn't just leave 'em laying for the vultures." Ron and LaDon acted surprised and Ron answered.

"Must 'a been dry-gulched or a hold up. Nice of 'em to tidy things up though. Might have been days before anyone knew of it or found him, just too bad!" Ron and the men got another drink and went to a table to sit. Kin Johnson stopped by their table and asked if they wanted a meal. "We got pork roast tonight, with taters and biscuits. Real tasty and filling it is." They all ordered a meal and played some cards while waiting to be served. They ate their meal gave Kim a tip and went to the bar to pay Mark.   The swinging doors flew open and a young man with a pistol on his hip charged in with hatred in his eyes. "You killed my brother did ya?" He challenged. Mark leaned over the bar and whispered to Ron. "That's Barry's younger brother, got my shotgun right behind your back if ya don't have a pistol, and it's cocked, be careful."

"Thanks," Ron said, "Might need it." He slid his left hand behind his back and grabbed the double barrel holding it place and said. "I didn't kill anyone boy, what you talking about?" The young man lowered his hand closer to his pistol. "I know you killed him because he told me he was riding out to see you and get his money back."

"So he was out to kill me was he? He was a cheating lowlife worthless varmint!" Ron returned. "I don't know who killed him. Now get your hand away from your gun, don't do anything foolish boy." With that the young man grabbed for his pistol. Ron quickly stuck the double barrel in front of him and pulled the triggers. There was a defining roar and it blew the young man back out the door with his feet off the floor. Ron quickly reloaded with two shells from Mark and looked around the room to see if there was any more trouble coming. When satisfied he returned the shotgun to Mark.

"Thanks pal," Ron said, "He would have drilled me if you hadn't helped."

"Glad to be able to help ya," Mark said with a smile, and put the gun back under the bar. Some of the patrons left to look at the dead young man on the side walk and things were quiet in the bar. Mark poured Ron a shot. Sheriff George Royal came in. "What's happened here?" He demanded. Mark leaned over the bar and told him what happened and that Ron had no choice but to do what he did in self defense. They talked it over and the sheriff was satisfied with the answers, and everyone's story in the saloon was the same. "You know anything about Barry Moore's death?" He asked Ron.

"No sheriff, I don't know how he got killed."

"You hear any shots fired today?" Ron looked at his men than at George. "No Sir....well wait a minute. I did hear a shot around four this afternoon and I saw a Injun' ride 'in off hard about fifteen minutes later. I just figured he shot a deer or elk or such."

"It's not very likely for an Indian to shoot a man and put him back on his horse," George replied, "If you hear of anything that could help me solve his death, let me know."

"Will do for sure sheriff," Ron answered, "If I hear of it I'll let you know for sure."

Sheriff Royal then asked a couple of men to help him get the body to the undertaker.

"Thanks For your help Mark," Ron said, "Come on boys, funs over for me. Let's ride back to the ranch." Mark smiled. "Glad to help Ron, hurry back."

Chapter Eighteen

Amber and I walked out into the street. Things were getting a little more quiet as people were getting settled for the night. The saloon near by was playing music and Amber seemed like she was getting into the rhythm wiggling her feet to the tunes. She had a smile on her face and a sparkle in her eyes. We walked to Leslie's rooming house and walked in. There were dining tables and soft furniture to sit on. It really was neat and clean. There were curtains on the windows and drapes on the doorway to the back. It really looked homey and inviting.

"Hello me darlings, can I be of help to you?" A lady asked as she came out from behind the drape. "My name is Leslie Montgomery, but you can call me Leslie and if there is anything I can do to make your stay in Batesville comfortable while you're here I aim to please. Good food, clean warm rooms, and no rowdy's to bother you." She was a friendly lady and seemed very warm and professional. "Yes Ma'am we want to stay the night, get something to eat, and a hot bath would be so nice." I answered.

"I can take care of all that young man," she said, "How long do you want to stay?"

"Just tonight ma'am, we will be leaving in the morning. Working a cattle drive to St. Louis and need to get back with supplies."

"St. Louis? Are you kidding? Nobody goes there with cattle anymore." Ms. Leslie proclaimed. "It's too dangerous, Indians, rustlers, and closed ranges. I don't see how you're going to do that."

"We have a route planned and checked it over." I answered. "We can do it. You're right it's not going to be easy, but we've planned it out well and so far we've had only a few problems."

"Well I wish you all the luck young man. Are you planning on eating with us tonight?" She asked. "Tonight it's roast chicken, mashed potatoes with gravy and greens. I serve dinner till nine."

"Yes ma'am we are but I think I will walk to a saloon and get me a shot."

"No need to do that, young man. I got the best whisky in town. All the way from New York it is and very good indeed."

"Great I'll have a shot or two. How about you Amber?"

"I don't really care much for whisky, Brad, but I could go for some brandy or wine if we can find some in town."

"Not to worry young lady. I got some very good red wine that came from New York also. I could chill it for you if you like." Miss Montgomery replied.

"Hope we can afford it with it coming all the way from New York with the price of freight these days." I answered.

"I said it came from New York, I didn't say I had shipped it in from there. Did some dealings with a man coming through town with a big wagon load of whisky and bottled wine. Don't know how he got it and didn't worry much about it. I could charge more but I don't for the right people." She said laughingly.

"Well that settles that," I answered, Want 'ta get a bath before hand Amber?"

"No I'll wash up a little and them we can have our drinks before dinner and I'll get my hot bath before going to bed, if that's O K?"

"That will be fine with me, sounds good. Miss Montgomery can you chill the wine for the lady?"

"Yes I can! You go wash up and I'll set a table for you, with a candle even. How's that?" She quizzed. This sounded real nice to me. A good meal, a couple of drinks and a nice time with a lovely lady.

"After dinner I'll have my helper have plenty of hot water for your bath in the wash house. You can bathe together or you can use two stalls. I have four tubs open."

"I think we will bathe separate." Amber answered with a smile. I chuckled.

"Now you youngins' get washed up and I'll get workin' on the details."

We asked about a room so we could put our belongings up.

"One room?" Miss Montgomery asked?

"Ma'am I think we will need two rooms." I answered.
"Brad, there's no sense wasting money. Miss Leslie do you
have a room with a bed for two?" Amber asked. I was
stunned. Didn't expect that. Things are looking up, I
thought. I can't believe she said that.
"Yes young lady I do. A real comfy bed too!" Was her
answer. Amber looked at me and smiled. She was blushing;
she looked so pretty with color in her face.
"Here's the key, room three. Go up the stairs and first
room on the right. Now go get washed up and I'll get things
set up for your evening."
Amber and I took our belongings up stairs to the room. It
wasn't a big room but space enough and was well laid out.
There was a wash basin and pitcher of water on the dresser
with soap and hand towels. Amber took a towel and said
she would go to the wash house and meet me downstairs.
The water was warm and it felt good so get the dust off my
face. I cleaned up and went down to meet Amber. Miss
Montgomery and a young lady brought a bottle of wine and
a bottle of whisky to our table and a glass for me with ice in
it, haven't seen that much. Amber sat down and the young
lady un-corked the wine bottle and poured Amber
a glass full. I opened the whisky a poured me a drink. This
was so nice, a lit candle, drinks and I'm sure a good meal to
boot. People were sitting at other tables with smiles. They
must have thought of us as newly-weds.

"This is my niece, Jessica Trombini," she said, "She helps me here and will be taking care of your needs with me tonight. She will also check you out tomorrow morning as I have to take my buckboard to Willow Springs Missouri on some business."

"Are you going by yourself?" I asked. "No, my darling there's a cavalry unit in town and I will pull out early morning with them. Don't dare go it alone with all the Indian attacks take-in' place lately. It's much too dangerous and, the chance of highway men trying to rob you is great also. You will need to be alert also on the trail catching up to your group."

"Thanks we will keep our eyes open." I replied. "You can ride with us if you want." Miss Montgomery offered.

"We won't be leaving until after nine. You'll be long gone by then Ma'am." We sat and talked sipping on our drinks. "Brad, I'm so glad you let me come with you." Amber said looking at me with her eye's smiling. "I enjoy being with you and your company. I can get used to this. Hope I'm not being to forward."

"Not at all Miss Amber, I enjoy being with you and getting to know you too."

"That's real nice, Brad, thank you."

Miss Jessica told us to let her know when we were ready for dinner. I asked her how long she had been working at the hotel.

"About a year now," she answered, "Aunt Leslie took me in after my Mom and Dad were killed by an Indian attack at our farm just out side of town last year."

"Was your Dad and Mom from around these parts?" I Quizzed.

"No it was about twenty five years ago my Dad came here from Italy and met my Mom, Aunt Leslie's sister, and settled near here."

"Sorry to hear of you trouble Jessica, glad you were safe though." She smiled and told us that she enjoyed working with her Aunt Leslie and she had extra income from a man who was leasing the farm from her and her deed of ownership was free and clear.

"Maybe some day I'll find the right man and move back on the farm, but not in any hurry though." Amber and I continued chatting, sipping our drinks; it was a very enjoyable evening. We ordered our dinner and ate all we wanted. It was a very good meal and Miss Leslie brought us some coffee and cake for dessert. "On the house," she said with a smile. We finished our cake and coffee and Miss Leslie came to our table. "Hope you enjoyed it folks." I looked up and thanked for all she did and told her Amber and I was ready to hit the bath house.

"Keep the bottles for the trail, you paid for them as far as

I'm concerned." she
replied, "Thank you for staying with us. I'll get the hot
water ready. Hope you sleep well and have a safe trip." We
thanked her again. It has been a long time since I've had
such an enjoyable night. We went to the wash house and I
asked Amber if she needed any help with a grin on my
face.
"I'll do just fine thank you Brad. I think I can figure it out
O K." She smiled and went inside. I got into my tub of hot
water and just soaked it in. My how good it felt to relax. I
could hear Amber singing in her bath. She was loving it
too!

Chapter Nineteen

I laid in the tub for a quite a while, then I finished washing up. It was so wonderful and I enjoyed every minute of it. As I was drying myself off I was wondering how this was going to turn out, with us sleeping together and all. I still couldn't believe she would be so forward. I'm sure she hasn't done this before, I thought to myself. She has been such a proper straight lady up to this point. But she said she has never slept with a man before. Confused I was, puzzled. I went to the room wrapped in a big towel and got a shirt and undies' on and sat on a bench waiting for her. Shortly she came in with her new night shirt on. If she had anymore on I didn't know. She looked so refreshed and her skin was so pink and her eyes were sparkling. I lit a ready rolled smoke and leaned back and took in the sights so to speak. Amber sat on the edge of the bed and told me how great that bath had felt. I agreed. Then we got quiet. Now I was feeling tension, nervous, not sure what to say next. She took a drink from her wine bottle. Building up courage I thought to myself. I grabbed my bottle of whisky and downed a good shot myself. Not a bad idea I thought.
"Well I guess we need to hit the sack." I suggested "We need to get some rest."
"Brad, I want you to know," she said with authority, "All we are going to do is sleep comfortably. Snuggling is O K

but that's it!" I looked her in the eyes and her whole demeanor had changed and she was nervous.

"Sure, I mean of course by all means." I answered.

"I promised my dad that I wouldn't give myself to no man unless we were married. I am going to keep my promise Brad. It's not that I don't want you, It's I can't. I must keep my promise to him. Do you understand?"

"Yes I do Amber; I didn't expect anything, just a good night's sleep."

"You don't want me?" She said, and her eyes turned to a glare.

"Yes I do, but I will not do anything that you don't want nor do I want to hurt you or our relationship. I respect your wishes. I can sleep on the floor, that will be fine. I'll sleep OK there"

"No you're not! You're going to sleep in the bed and keep me warm but that's all till we marry!" Suddenly she had the look of embarrassment. "Oh I didn't mean to say that, we haven't even discussed that yet. I feel ashamed of myself now. Being so forward. I don't know if you would want to marry me. I mean…."

"That's OK. Any man would be proud to be your husband, including me." Well I sure put myself in the ring didn't I? "Cover up and move over sweetheart, we need some rest." I could tell she felt bad and was worrying about how I was feeling. I blew out he light and crawled in the bed with my back towards her. It was a comfortable bed, and it felt so good to lie in a bed, instead of wrapping up in a blanket on the ground. I laid there for a while wondering what she was thinking. Next thing I know she was snuggling up to me with her arm around my waist and her warm body pressed tightly to mine. My head was spinning.

"Good night Brad," she whispered, "Thank you for understanding and please forgive me for being so forward." She then kissed me on the back of my neck. After a while she rolled over and I snuggled up to her with my arm around her and my leg over hers. She was so soft, so warn and her fragrance filled my nostrils. I was really getting warm, I mean warm! I laid there holding her for dear life like a coyote with a rabbit in his jaws. I haven't felt like this in a long time! She wiggled and pushed her body tighter to me. I'm going nuts; my head is in a spin. This is torture. How long can I endure this? I laid there. Getting warmer by the minute and my blood pressure was going sky high. Suddenly I jumped out of bed and started to put my pants and shirt on.

"Get up," I said as I lit the lamp, "Get up and get dressed." Amber looked at me confused.

"What?" She asked. "What's the matter?"

"Just get up and get your clothes on woman, now." I said. She got up and went behind a changing panel and put her clothes on. She came out and I could see she was confused and nervous.

"What on earth is going on Brad?" I put my boots on and grabbed her hand and pulled her out the door and down the stairs. It was late but Miss Montgomery and Jessica were finishing cleaning up for the night.

"Is something wrong?" She asked.

"I need a preacher man. Where can I find one? We're getting married. I mean Now!" Amber looked at me with a shocked look on her face. "Brad, are you serious?"

"Oh yes I am Lady, if you'll have me that is." She threw her arms around me and gave me a kiss like none I've had before.

Miss Leslie told me; "I'm a justice of the peace, I can do it but I'll need you to fill out a marriage license. And Jessica can be a witness."

"Where are the papers? Let's get em' filled out." I demanded. "Lets get the show on the road!" Miss Leslie got the papers and I grabbed them and filled out my part and I handed them to Amber to fill her section. She was smiling and kept hold of my arm, and kissing me on the neck and I kissed back. What a sight we must have been. Miss Montgomery read the scripture and made it official and handed me the bill for the license and registration.

"Congratulations you two, you make a lovely wonderful couple." She said and hugged me and Amber. I turned and gave Amber a long heavy kiss. Then I said, "O K woman, now get upstairs and get those clothes off!" Miss Montgomery's eyes went as large as pool balls and her mouth was wide open. Jessica blushed at my remark. Amber looked at me with the devil her eyes and replied, "I'm going up to our room Mr. Lassiter, and when you come up lets see if your man enough to get these clothes off!"

Miss Montgomery's mouth went wide open again in astonishment and Jessica's eyes were big as silver dollars. I paid for the marriage license, registration papers and the wedding service and went upstairs to the room.

Chapter Twenty

I awoke at daybreak and looked over at Amber. She was sound asleep. I rolled over and held her in my arms. She made cooing sounds and snuggled back. "Good morning Mrs. Lassiter." I said softly. "How are you this morning?" "Mr. Lassiter, I feel wonderful. I can't believe this can be true. I am so happy Brad. Thank you." She looked so lovely and felt so warm and soft. We engaged in a kiss that seemed to last for minutes. When we got out of bed we got some towels and clothes and went to the wash rooms. I opened the door to one of the stalls for her and as she went in she grabbed my arm and took me with her. Best bath I've ever had! We dressed and went into the main room. There were people eating breakfast and having coffee, quite busy.

"Good morning, sleep well?" Jessica asked. "Yes we did young lady. The bed felt so good and we were warm all night." Jessica blushed and asked. "Are you having breakfast? We have eggs and sausage, flap jacks with real butter, and syrup, you can have both if you like."

"I'll have both, how about you dear?" I asked Amber. She smiled. "I'll have the flap jacks with sausage. Did your Aunt get off OK Jessica?"

"Yes she did. They left about six this morning. It will take the most of two days to get to Willow Springs but at least I know she is in safe company traveling with the cavalry escort."

"I'm sure all will be just fine with her traveling with them." I replied.

"I'll get you some coffee while you're waiting for breakfast." Jessica said to us, "It won't take long at all the cook here is good and fast too!"

We ate a good breakfast and went to our room to get our belongings and went to the desk to pay the bill. The charges were very reasonable but I noticed something was missing.

"I don't see the wine or the whisky on the bill Jessica."

"Aunt Leslie told me to tell you it was a wedding gift. She also said to tell you she was happy to have married you and she wouldn't ever forget it." I thanked her and told her to thank her Aunt when she returned and that we wouldn't forget both of them either. We went to the stable, paid our fee, got our horses and the wagon and headed to Cliffs store.

"Good morning folks." Cliff greeted us, "I have all in order and if you will pull around back I will have my man help you load it up." We went to the back and got loaded up in no time and were ready to pull out of town.

"Thanks for your business, Mr. Lassiter. If you will go to the center of town," Cliff offered, "There's a road that goes north east straight to Walnut Ridge. You should pick up your cattle trail as you said, that's the way they were

heading. Keep alert though. The road is heavily traveled with freight wagons and prospectors so it's mostly safe going, but you never know. There's so much activity on the road the Indians don't bother it much. " I paid Cliff and thanked him for all his help and after stopping at the post office to send my Mom and Patti a telegram, we started on our way. Amber sat as close as she could get next to me and kept
patting and squeezing me on the leg. The road was in good shape and we did see a
lot of wagons going both ways. The country was open and we saw a lot of wildlife, deer, elk, antelope and a jack rabbit here and there. We traveled until about one in the afternoon when we came to a camp of what looked like hunters or trappers. About six men were sitting around a small fire drinking coffee. I pulled up cautiously fore I was not sure if they were going to be friendly and told Amber to hold her rifle in her hands just to be ready. One of them stood up and walked toward us. He had a smile on his face and didn't look threatening.

"Howdy folks, want-ta' use our far?" He asked. "We's were gettin' ready to leave soon anyway. Youin' be welcome if yaw' be needin' it."

"Thank you sir, we can warm some bread, cheese and make coffee." I answered. "Mighty warm of you to offer."

"Got coffee made, no need ta fix none as dare's plenty in da pot."

I told Amber to keep her eyes open just in case, but they turned out to be a very friendly group of men and tipped their hats to Amber and each shook my hand and identified themselves.

"Have you men seen a cattle drive in your travels heading north?" I asked.

"Yesterday we past 'em. Big herd, ain't seen none like that in a long time." One man said. "They said dey were going to go tight west of the town of Walnut Ridge. We stopped and had lunch wid 'em, day were mite friendly folks."

"That's my Dads herd, going to St. Louis."

"Dat's what day said," He replied, "I told dem I dint know bout none cattle comin' from Texas went dare no more."

"I couldn't believe it either when my dad told me he was making this drive. But he seems to have it all worked out." We warmed some bread and cheese and knawel on some jerky. The coffee was so strong you could paint with it. The men went about packing up so I gave them their pot and thanked them for their hospitality.

"Yer mighty welcome folks," The man replied, "Just be on the look out fer Injuns when you get past the town of Pocahontas all da way inta' South Mozori. Been a heap a trouble up dat way. Mostly mixed renegades' from several tribes banded up."

166

"Thanks for the warning, and thanks for the use of your fire." We shook hands and he tipped his hat to Amber. I put out the fire and we got back on the wagon to head on. About an hour later we came across the trail of our herd so we started following it. We were making good time and we hadn't stayed too long for lunch. Amber would give me a peck on the cheek every now and then. "Brad, have I told you I love you?" She asked. "Yes you did and I love you too! I'm a lucky man."

"How long will it take to catch up with our group?" Amber asked.

"It will most likely be after night fall as long as we can follow the herds trail in the darkness." I replied. "I think we have a little moon tonight, which will be a help. We'll just have to see how it goes. I would rather catch up with them instead of making camp out here alone."

Amber nodded. "I hope we can also, Brad, we haven't seen anyone since we caught up to the herds trail."

It started to get dark as the sun went over the hills. I asked Amber if she wanted to stretch her legs a little. "Yes," she answered, "That would be nice to take a minute and get the kinks out." We got down from the wagon and went different directions to check out the bushes so to speak. There was some moonlight so we could see pretty well. I rolled a smoke and we took a drink from our canteens. Felt good to walk a little and get some circulation moving in our legs.

We climbed back on the wagon and headed on. For a while I could see the lights from the town of Walnut Ridge off to the east lighting up the sky. About an hour later, maybe a little more, I could see a large campfire ahead of us. I was hoping it was our camp, but the size of the fire worried me. This was a very large campfire. I pulled the reins and stopped the team.

"Hon, I want you to stay here with the wagon." I told Amber. "I'm going to creep up and see if I can make out who has that fire." Amber asked me to be careful. I didn't take a horse as I didn't want it to winnie and give my position away. I slowly snuck up as close as I wanted with out being seen. I was glad I did. It was a large band of renegade Indians and they were drinking whisky. A bad mix as Indians didn't hold liquor well. They were hooping, chanting and dancing around the fire. This is not good, I thought. We must turn back some before we try to go around them. I was very concerned for Ambers safety, if they found me I didn't have a chance and if they found her she might as well shoot herself. That would be the most humane thing she could do. As I started to sneak back to her and the wagon I saw someone's outline next to some junipers. I pulled out my knife to defend myself. I couldn't shoot, that would be the end for sure.

"Sssshh," the figure said as it motioned me toward him.
Thanks almighty it was A K!

"Let's get back to the wagon," he said," I'll lead you out of
here to our camp. It's about five miles from here on the
other side of the Mesa. Be very quiet." I was so glad it was
him. He said he was looking for me because he knew I
should be closing in on our camp soon. While scouting
ahead of the drive earlier in the day he found the Indian
camp when they were north east of Pocahontas. They drove
around the back side of the Mesa to avoid the Indians.

"They won't be trouble tonight," A K said," But they will
be in a foul mood tomorrow. We need ta' pull out early and
get away from them. No squaws in their camp so it's a war
or raiding party."

"Do you think they know of the cattle drive yet A K?" I
asked.

"No, they came from the west, no see us yet. Let's get
moving."

I got in on the wagon and I could see Amber was afraid.
"It'll be O K Hon," I told her, "A K will get us out of here
O K. Don't worry."

She looked at me and said. "I am in fear Brad! A K came to
me before he found you and told me what was happening.
He gave me this bottle and told me if I hear shooting to
pour it all over me to run and hide." I looked at the little

bottle and asked what it was. She handed it to me. I pulled the cork.

"Whoa," I said, "Smells like skunk."

"A K said the Indians would think so also and not come near me thinking I was a skunk and they wouldn't want to get sprayed."

"Well I glad you didn't have to use it or you would be riding in the back of the wagon."

I chuckled. That A K is really a special friend and a fine shrewd Sioux warrior.

Chapter Twenty One

We started off in an easterly direction. A K had cut some small cedars trees to drag behind the wagon and cover our tracks. His thinking was if our trail was found by the Indians they wouldn't see the wagon tracks and think it was just some mountain men or a small cavalry detachment passing though and not follow us to camp or our cattle trail. In a short time we were at our camp. The men and my Dad came to meet us. I was so glad we made it safely.

"Good to see you Son," my Dad proclaimed, "Have any trouble?"

"No dad we did just fine and I got all the goods that Cookie and the men asked for. I sent a telegram to Mom telling her we were doing well and to reply us at West Plains Missouri and we would pick up her answer there."

"Good job Son, you did a good job."

"Dad I have a surprise for you." He looked at me with a raised eyebrow.

"What's that Brad?" He asked.

"I want you to meet Mrs. Lassiter, and I told Mom also." When I told him that, he had a look of warm surprise in his eyes.

"Well Son, you let your heart lead you and I am happy for you. You made a fine choice and I welcome her to our family." With that he gave Amber a big hug.

"Welcome to the family young lady," He said with a big grin, "Proud to have you part of us!"

"Thank you so much Mr. Lassiter, I am a very happy girl." Amber said to him.

"Girl hell," Dad replied, "You're a fine young woman, and Miss Becky will be so overjoyed. Welcome to the family."

It didn't take long for the news to get around to the men and they came to Amber and I to give their best regards. The men helped Cookie John get his supplies transferred to his wagons and put in place I gave them the items they asked me to get for them and they were like kids at Christmas. My brother Steve came riding up and stopped his horse in front of us. He ran over to Amber and gave her a big hug and welcomed her to our family. He then gave me a hug picking me off the ground.

"Congratulations Brad," He said, "She's a fine addition to the family my brother.

Amber, if he treats you wrong let me know and I'll kick his butt."

"I don't feel that will be ever necessary Steve, he's a true gentleman. I'm the one that's lucky."

"Kick my butt Steve." I said. He looked at me and answered.

"I outweigh you by a hundred pounds. I'll just sit on ya' and let her kick your tail." We laughed and hugged again. It was so good to be back with friends and family.

"OK folks," Cookie hollered, "We are going to have a wedding celebration tonight. I got me a hog on the fire and I am going to make a cornbread honey wedding cake. The best yall' ever did have." He brought out a keg of whisky and told all to take a swig or two and pass it around. He made good smooth whisky. Even Amber took a swallow!

John had shot a nice size hog earlier in the day and put on a spit over the fire. He mixed his cornbread in a big Dutch oven and set it next to the coals. Jeff Cushing came to me and offered his good tidings. I was glad he was with us. We spent a long time in the wilderness together in the cavalry and he was like a brother to me. A true friend indeed. We fought and chased down Indians, rustlers and outlaws in our service with the cavalry, both getting wounded in our doings.

We ate a real good meal and the corn bread cake was really tasty. The men kept congratulating Amber and I as we all sat by the fire. I pulled out a ready rolled smoke and lit it. The men thought that was really something. Some thought I rolled them earlier and put them in a box. A K stood up and asked for our attention

"We need to get some rest," He said, "We will need to get up early and be ready. Those renegades' will be huntin' trouble tomorrow. Have your weapons ready while watching the herd and those sleeping, sleep light and with your guns. I will sneak out and see if I can figure what their

173

going to do. Steve will be just out side camp on guard. It would be good to have a man on the other side of camp also. Good night." He waved and mounted his horse and rode off.

I bought a tarp from Cliffs store and with a couple of short poles it made a nice lean-to next to the fire for Amber and me to sleep under. It also collected the heat from the fire to keep her warm. I gave her a hug and a kiss and mounted up on Prince to take my shift. The cattle were in large blind end box canyon that had plenty of grass for them to graze. It made it real easy to control them as there was only one way out. The nights were becoming a lot more chilly the further north we moved and tonight was no exception. I had a blanket thrown over my shoulders and I was glad I brought it. It was a clear night and a full moon. You could hear coyotes and wolves howling in the hills. I heard a cougar scream and that quieted things up for a while. Dead silence. I was hoping A K wouldn't run into any problems, he was sharp warrior, but I worry just the same. Buddy Perryman, Lee Tingy and John Butler were riding herd with me. There wasn't much to do as the canyon opening was small and easy to keep them in unless something frightened them.

"Did you hear that cougar cry?" Buddy asked.

"Yes I did," I answered, "Sounds like a woman screaming."

"Sure does, make my hair stand up. I hope he doesn't get in to the herd Brad. Those cattle will come out 'a there like buckshot from a double barrel."

"You right about that Buddy, we don't need them to stampede." So far we only had one stampede and I wasn't looking for any more of them. I could tell the men were a little tense, but not so much of the lion, but the possibility of Indian trouble. A K said they wouldn't be trouble until day break and he's always right when it come to guessing Indians. We rode back and forth listening and watching. But all was quiet.

Matt Yeaton, John Butler, Don Volsch and Joe Palmer came riding up to relieve us and we told them about the cougar and that it had only screamed once. They said they would keep their eyes and hears open and we rode back to camp. I took Prince to the tie line that Carlon had set up. I rolled a smoke and sat by the fire for a while. I finished my smoke and crawled under the fly with Amber. She asked if she needed to ride herd and I told her that the men had taken care of that. I snuggled up to her warm body and fell asleep.

The next morning Cookie had breakfast and coffee ready. Corn beef and biscuits. We sat next to the fire and it felt good. Steve said he heard or saw nothing during the night. That was good news. A K came riding up and told us the Indians moved out early and headed due north. "Don't let your guard down," He said," They might swing our way and that would be trouble. Mix of Sioux, Kiowa and Comanche's and they be wearing war paint. Make sure your guns are loaded and be ready for trouble" We thanked him and he rode off in the direction of our drive plan. I wondered if he ever slept.

Chapter Twenty Two

"RO-L-L-L-L 'Em Out!" Arnie bellowed and we started
moving the herd out of the canyon moving north. The
Buffalo was still in the herd but he was up in the front now
acting as a boss bull. With the strays and wild cattle we
picked up along our drive the herd number was to thirty
eight hundred now. I saw Matt Barnes with Rick and Harry
and they spread out along the herd on the west side with
several other riders. Amber was behind me and the rest of
the men and the Vaqueros moved forward to circle the
cattle to keep them together and narrow them out as we
headed them north. We tried to string them out some in a
line about sixty to seventy cattle wide as we didn't want
them in a ball. It had warmed up quickly, that felt so good.
The sky several miles ahead looked like a storms a coming.
We were almost into Missouri best I could figure from
what Dad had said. The cattle were moving along at a good
pace. Arnie told me we were making good time and were a
couple of days ahead. The average going so far was about
fourteen to fifteen miles per day. Luckily we have had good
water and grass along the trail so there wasn't any weight
loss. A K had planned a very good trail. The ground was
flat and had prickly pear cactus growing in groups here and
there. I put my gloves on and picked a few to take back to
camp. They have a lot of seeds in them but have a sweet

taste to them. The ground was open with some brush and small juniper and mesquite trees. The trail was taking us to a draw between two mountain ranges and the storm caught up with us. I threw my slicker over me and checked to see if Amber had hers and she had it over her. We moved along in the rain and had some thunder and lighting. Every once and a while several cows would bolt but we were able to keep the herd together. We didn't need a stampede. We slogged along for an hour or so with the rain coning down hard at times. As it was getting to mid day the rain subsided and then it was gone. In no time at all with the sun back out the heat returned. Time for a nooner' soon, some food and coffee would be nice. I saw Cookie John's wagons ahead and he was busy making lunch. Some of the men rode forward and brought the cattle to a halt so they could spread out and graze. Some of them started eating the fruit from the Prickly Pear cactus. The rain had soaked into the ground quickly and you would have never known it had rained except for what was on the brush and the leaves. It got real humid fast. I threw off my slicker and tethered Prince to a bush. Amber rode up.

"Got lucky," She said, "I was afraid they were going to bolt when that thunder started."

"Me too, but we held them in pretty well. Did you stay mostly dry?"

"Ya, mostly, I'll dry out quickly. Ready for some coffee?"

"Yes I am." We went over and got some coffee. Cookie said, "It'll be ready in a minute folks, almost done it is."
"What are we having?" Amber asked.
"Surprise stew and tortillas patties my lady." John replied.
"What's surprise stew Cookie?" Amber quizzed. I told her just don't ask, just eat. She gave me a puzzled look and stared into the pot. John was flipping tortillas and piling then up.
"Dig in," He hollered, and the men got in line. John threw a patty on their plates and a scoop of stew to roll up. Amber stood there and looked at hers.
"Honey it's good," I said, "John knows his stuff."
"Maybe so Brad, but I don't know what's in his stuff." She slowly raised it to her mouth and took a bite. Her eyebrows raised a little. "It tastes good, but I sure would like to know what I'm eating." I laughed and went back for another. Knowing John it could be rattlesnake, ground gopher, turtle or coyote meat or all but it was good and filling. When he said surprise I knew it wasn't deer, elk, hog or turkey.
 I looked up in the sky and saw several vultures circling about a mile off. A K saw them too.
"I'm going to have a look, Brad." He said, "Just being curious." He climbed into the saddle and trotted off in the direction of the swarm. I got me another coffee, rolled a smoke and talked with the men and Amber. In no time at

all A K came back, his horse flat out in a run. He pulled up and said.

"Brad, grab four or five men and come with me" He had a serious look on his face. I turned and looked at the men at hand.

"Matt, Rick, Harry, Mr. Witt and Jeff mount up and follow me." They climbed into their saddles and we rode off in the direction of A K. As I got about a half mile I could see a Conestoga wagon with four oxen sitting ahead. The wagon had several arrows sticking out of it and bullet holes in the canvas. There was the body of a man, who had been scalped, lying next to the wagon. He was dead for sure.

"Brad I think it was the war party we've been a watching." A K said. We checked the man and he was dead for sure. My men all had their rifles out for the ready now. A K rode to the wagon and pointed. "Brad there is a lady lying across the seat." He climbed up to check her. "She's wounded but alive," He hollered, "Let's get her out on the ground." Jeff and Matt helped A K get her pulled out of the wagon and laid her on Jeff's slicker. She had a wound on the side of her head but it did look very serious. It just knocked her out. She was bleeding some but not too bad. Witt walked up and a look of complete surprise covered his face. "Good Lord," He proclaimed, "That's Miss Harris! I know her, I'm sure that's her." We all looked at Mr. Witt with surprise on our faces. "I spent some time at her father's farm in South Carolina a few years back. Helped him build a coral and herded up some cattle for him before I headed to Wyoming Territory. Why is she out here?"

Harry poured some water from his canteen on the wound and wiped it with a hanky from his pocket. She opened her eyes and stared at us in confusion. A K said it didn't look like they took anything from the wagon. That puzzled him. I looked at the man on the ground. They had taken the mans pistol and gun belt. If he had a rifle that was gone too!

Miss Harris sat up and looked around holding her head. "Ce Ce, where's my Ce Ce?" She screamed. "Where's my Ce Ce? Is she safe? Where is she?" I asked her who she was asking for. "My Grand daughter, Ce Ce. Is she alright?"

"There no one in the wagon," A K replied, "That's why they left in such a hurry. They took her grand daughter and hi-tailed it. I'll locate their trail." There was blood on the ground hopefully from wounded Indians and not the girl. Lee Tingy rode up with Amber. "Let's put her in the wagon, Lee said, "I'll drive it back to camp and have Cookie John look at her wound."

"Thanks Lee. Amber you go back with Lee." I said. "I'll stay here with the men till we figure out what happened to the girl." They put Miss Harris in the wagon and she was still calling for Ce Ce.

"I'll help John," Amber told me, "Maybe we can get her calmed down some." I waved to her and she rode back to camp with the wagon.

"I found their trail, looks like there's wounded in the bunch." A K confirmed. "You men wait at camp. Keep a look out, they might return for that wagon. I'm gonna' have a look and see what I can find out. Just sit tight till I get back."

We buried the man and marked his grave the best we could. He had a couple of arrows and some bullet holes in him. He must have put up a good fight. When we got back to camp Miss Harris was crying and sobbing for Ce Ce.

"I can't believe it," Mr. Witt said, "What is she doing all the way out here?" I assured him I didn't have any idea. Miss Harris looked up and saw Mr. Witt.

"Richard, Richard Witt,' she exclaimed, "Is that you Witt."

"Yes Ma'am it is. Sorry to see you get hurt Ma'am."

"I'll be all right, just knocked out for a while. Any sign of my granddaughter?"

"One of our men is looking for her Miss Harris." Witt answered. "He'll find where she is. Don't you worry none. We'll get her back to you."

"Oh I pray you do. She's only twenty and so innocent. I pray you find her safe."

John gave her a watered down shot of whisky and some coffee. She told us she hired the man we found, Mr.

Barrow, to drive her wagon to Oklahoma for the last land grab that was taking place on September sixteenth, about a month or so from now. She and her granddaughter were going to stake out some land in Oklahoma to start a farm and a new life.

Miss Harris said they were attacked by about twenty or more Indians and Mr. Barrow was shooting his shotgun and Ce Ce was using his pistol and she didn't remember anything more after the shot to her head knocked her out.

"Richard you never wrote back to me. What happened?"

"I got with my clan and helped them out Miss Harris. After that was taken care of I started drifting and got caught up with the west Ma'am. I meant to write and thought of you a lot though!"

"I figured you must have been killed or maybe found some woman and married."

"Naw' Ma'am no such thing. Just got lost out there, took in the sights. Sorry, I did mean to write and then I figured you done got hitched yer' self." Miss Barbara shook her head and wiped tears from her face. Mr. Witt and Miss Harris sat and talked for quite a while. He held her hand and did his best to calm her.

A K came back to camp.

"Found them," he said, "Bout twenty or so. Dint' see the young in'. Most likely she's being held in one of the shelters. I'll get her back tonight. Gonna need some help though."

"Just tell us what you need," I answered, "Give ya all the help we can. Hope she's O K."

"I got a plan that I think will work if I can pull it off sure nuff'." A K said. "Gotta' change my looks though." A K put on a pair buckskin trousers and moccasins he had. He then asked Cookie John to borrow his Buffalo hide vest and two big bottles of wine. John gladly gave them to him. He then took off his hat and tied a bandana around his hair, put his gun belt and pistol on and put his knife behind his back.

"I want to meet them just before it gets dark." He told us. "I want you to follow me to a point and wait for me to return with the girl. Be ready to ambush em' as all hell is going to break loose." While he finishes getting ready I got Jeff, Matt Barnes, Mr. Witt, John Butler, Howard Branden, Trent Arthur and the strangers Rick and Harry together with me.

"Make sure your rifles and pistols are fully loaded." I ordered. "I've picked yall because I'm sure of your gun skills. Now if any does not wish to be part of this fight tell me now and I will ask for a man to replace you." I looked at the men and they all gave thumbs up in reply. "Thanks men, I appreciate your help."

A K came to us and said,

"Let's ride. We need to have all in place quickly and as quiet as we can." We rode out at a walk, not talking but very alert. As we got out some distance and near the Indian camp A K pointed at area with some very large boulders scattered around big enough to hide the men on their horses. "Wait here and be ready" A K said, "I will ride right through these boulders. Wish me luck." We waved and he rode toward the Indian camp. The men got in place and tried to keep the horses quiet as they could smell the Indians and didn't care for it much.

A K rode to the camp and several of the Indians stood up and faced him weapons ready.

"Greetings brothers," A K announced in Sioux language, "I am Akecheta Otaktay of the Oglala Sioux." One of the tribe's men stepped forward.

"Greetings brother. That means Warrior That Kills Men. I am Sly Wolf, Lakota tribe. You ride white mans horse." A K got down and replied.

"Killed the man that owned it, needed ride. One less white man to deal with." Sly Wolf put his hand out.

"Yes too many whites now. Is there any end to them brother. Come join us, eat." A K tethered his horse next to the other horses on a rope line stretched between two aspens. He then reached into the saddle bags and brought out the two large bottles of wine and handed it to

Sly Wolf who pulled the cork and took a drink and passed them along.

"Nice gift brother," He said, "Very nice to share. We thank you." A K waved and went to the fire and cut some meat from a deer roasting over it and sat down. All the others were passing the wine and drinking it up quickly. A K just shook his head and grinned. He knew that it would help his plan. He sat for a while talking with the tribe members. He could tell they accepted him and he knew the alcohol would dull their minds quickly.

Chapter Twenty Three

A K sat by the fire and kept an eye on the goings on while talking with a tribe member. They were a mix of Sioux and Comanche's and they seemed to trust him. Finally he saw what he was looking for. One of them brought out a young girl with long blond hair. Her arms were tied at her wrist with leather and she was not being very cooperative kicking at the Indian that lead her to the fire. He sat her down and pulled some deer meat off and tried to get her to eat it and she wouldn't.

"Fiery white squaw," A K said, "She for sale?"

"No sale," Sly Wolf answered, "She will be gift to our Chief who's at other camp five miles from here." A K didn't like the sound of that.

"How many at camp?" He asked. "Ninety or so. We meet with them at early morning. Chief will like her." That's a hundred or so warriors A K thought, we are in for a tough fight when the girl is taken back. A K's thought we are going to need more help but from where? Wasn't long before the wine quieted things down and the Indians were hitting their blankets and robes. A K sat next to Ce Ce and she looked at him with contempt and hatred.

"I am here to save you," he whispered, "You must do as I say if you want to see your Grandma Harris again."

"You speak English," She said with surprised look, "Who are you? How do you know my Grand Mom?" A K whispered the details and what the Lassiter men are doing to help her.

"You must trust me, I work for the Lassiter ranch" A K told her, "Your life and mine depends on it." Ce Ce nodded her head. The warrior that was to watch her told A K to move away form the girl.

"I'll be back soon." He told her and walked away. A K eased back out of sight and watched the camp. After a short time the warrior that was watching her feel asleep sitting next to her. A K scanned the group and all of them seemed to be sleeping from drinking the wine. Time to make his move he thought. A K snuck up behind the guard very quietly. One more look to see if he wasn't noticed he made his move. He put his left hand over the brave's mouth, pulled his head back and cut his throat. He held him until he went lifeless then scalped him. Ce Ce nearly fainted at the sight of such horror and blood. A K quickly cut the bindings on her wrists and told her to be very quiet. "I want you to run with me to my horse. Don't trip please. Are you ready?" She nodded her head in agreement. He grabbed her hand and whispered, lets go and they ran as quiet as they could to his horse. He jumped into the saddle and pulled her up behind him. "Hang on tight." He ordered, and he eased the horse slow for a few yards then gave it a kick in the side and off they went at full speed. Ce Ce held on for dear life and it meant her life for sure. The braves in camp heard the commotion and found their dead comrade by the fire and went crazy. Gathering their weapons they ran and jumped onto their ponies and gave chase. A K had his horse going at a full run and the warriors were coming at speed behind them hollering and shooting guns and arrows. He could see the boulders and headed straight for them. Ce Ce let out a wail and squeezed A K even tighter. At the same time A K felt a searing burn on his left side. He headed his horse right into the large rocks and the men were ready. The first brave to ride in was met with Mr. Witt's bull whip. He swung it out and it wrapped around the braves neck and Witt pulled him off his horse and shot him as he hit the ground. Matt Barnes, Rick and Harry opened up with rifle fire and three more Indians went down. Jeff Cushing and Howard Brandon hit two more. Trent Arthur and John Butler started throwing lead and two more came off their horses. I shot two with my colt but they didn't fall but slumped over their horses. The Indian were caught by complete surprise and took heavy losses. They quickly turned and withdrew with several wounded and leaving nine dead on the ground. We rode hard back to camp. When we got there my Dad and a lot of the men came to us and asked how it went.

"Killed nine, wounded several," I told them, "I don't think they will return tonight. What do you think A K?"

"Not tonight, I'm a thinking," A K answered, "but we will catch hell in the morning as I learned the main camp has almost a hundred men a few miles from here." He shook his head and continued. "They will most likely tend to their dead and wounded and hit us early in the morning."

"That's going to be hard to handle," Arnie said to my Dad, "Don't have the men to hold 'em off and the herds gonna get scattered."

"Somehow we have to hold 'em Arnie!" My Dad replied. Arnie just shook his head. I looked at the girl.

"You O K?' I asked as I noticed blood on her shirt. She showed me where a bullet creased her side and left a burn mark. She was very lucky.

"The blood must be from A K." She said. "It's not from me." A K had taken a hit from the same bullet. It went through the skin on his left side but didn't do any serious damage, just a clean hole. He was cleaning it and put some flour and salt on it to stop the blood flow. Ce Ce went to her grandmom.

"Me Ma, are you all right?" She asked and gave her a big hug.

"Just a bad scratch on the head sweetheart. Did the Indians hurt or harm you?"

"No Me Ma, I bit and kicked them all I could." Miss Harris was so happy to see her granddaughter alive and safe. She gave A K a big hug and the red man turned even redder.

"Glad we could get her back Ma'am." A K said, "I hope you lady's can shoot a gun. We are going to need all the help we can get."

As we were trying to come up with a plan two Conestoga wagons pulled with oxen came rolling in with three ladies a man and two youngins', a boy and a girl. "Hi 'ya folks," the man called, "Can we camp with you tonight. I hear there's Indians on the war path and we would feel safer with you if it wouldn't be any bother on you."

My Dad and I walked over to meet them.

"I don't know how safe it's gonna' be." Dad said to them. "We just fought off a bunch and are expecting to be attacked in the morn."

"My son and I can shoot if that's a help." He answered. "I got a 45-70 carbine and about fifty round of ammo. Can you lend my son a weapon? He can handle a rifle well."

"Young man we need all the help we can get." Dad replied. "The problem is we are expecting over one hundred or more to attack us." The mans face went blank and his mouth opened. He looked around at his family then turned back to my Dad

"Sir, my name is Brother Billy Roberts." He then pointed and continued, "That's my Mother, Sister Dorothy Roberts, my Grandmother Sister Dorothy Hartman, my Wife, Sister Rebecca and my daughter Jasmin and my son Cameron."
"Nice to meet you folks, my name is Charlie Lassiter, the owner of this outfit. I'm not sure how this is going to turn out but, we're glad to have you and you'll be no trouble at all." Billy looked around with a serious look on his face like he was in deep thought.
"Mr. Lassiter, I think I got a plan for you." He offered. "When we were in West Plains I noticed an army post, Fort John Rollins near there. If you can lend me a horse I can be there in a little more than an hour and a half. I'm sure the Cavalry would able to send enough men to help and defend us."
A K came over to them.
"Boss," he said, "the mans got a good plan there. Have Carlon saddle him a horse and let 'em ride."
"Young man you may have just saved the day so to speak. Let's get you on your way." Dad told him.
"Boss," A K said, "As he's riding back to the fort lets get the herd moving toward West Plains. That way the Cav won't have that far to come help us."
"Alright," Dad said, "Lets get ready to move out. Arnie, get the herd moving North West to West Plains. The rest of ya'll let's get pack 'in."

Twenty Four

 It seemed like a good plan indeed. Moving the cattle herd
toward West Plains the Indians wouldn't find us setting
where they last saw us and would have to head north to
catch up with us to attack. By then the U.S. Cavalry should
be with us. Ce Ce said she could handle driving Miss
Harris's wagon and Lee Tingy took charge of one of the
Roberts wagons and Mrs. Rebecca Roberts said she could
handle the other one. We moved the herd north west and
the wagons followed. It was a good clear night a slight chill
in the air and the cattle were frisky and moving at a good
pace. It was in no time at all we were crossing the White
River. Dad said he thought it wouldn't take young Bill
Roberts more than an hour to reach West Plains as Bill was
thinking how long it took with his wagons pulled by the
oxen. A man on a horse would make it a lot quicker. The
river crossing went smoothly and the wagons didn't have
any trouble either. About an hour into the move we could
see the lights of West Plains in the distance. It was a relief
to see those lights. We kept moving at a good pace and
finally my Dad said, "Ride and tell the men to hold the herd
here. There's good water and plenty of grass. We are close
to the town and we will need daylight to go around it." I got

a couple of men near me and told them to ride to the front of the herd and tell Arnie the drive boss of dad's plan. Amber and I rode around the back of the herd to tell the men there.

"Get you wagons set and get ta cook in." Dad hollered to John Boger. We had stopped the herd and in about twenty minutes later James Harrell came riding up with a big smile on his face.

"Brad the Cav is here," He said, "Bout a hundred and fifty troopers."

"Thanks James," I replied, "That's great news. We really need them, glad we could get them to help." I feel more relieved now. If the Indians hit us without them the herd would be scattered from here to hell. John got to setting up for our evening meal and we were sure hungry and ready for a rest. Dad and I rode to meet the troopers and Bill Roberts was riding in front with them. We thanked him for his help and told him that he and his family were to join us for the evening meal. He said it wasn't necessary but we insisted. As the troopers came up I recognized the officer leading them. It was Chuck Munson, Jeff and I had served with him. He was wearing the rank of Captain.

"Howdy Captain," I said as I saluted him, "See you've made some advance in rank since I saw 'ya."

"Brad Lassiter, is that you for sure?" He asked with a big smile on his face.

"Your lookin' good my friend. How's it been with you and your lovely wife Judy? Got any youngins' yet?" I looked at him sadly and lowered my head for a second.

"I lost her some time back Chuck."

"So sorry to hear that Brad, my condolences' to you."

"It was tough, Chuck, it really was, but I dealt with it the best I could and I recently remarried and we are happy. She's a great lady."

"Glad to hear that pal. Glad you found someone. Good for you!

I'll get to talk with you Brad about updates at a better time. But for now let me tell you of my plan for handling this situation."

"OK Chuck." I replied. "Tell what you got in mind."

"You did well Brad by moving close to town and I am sure the Indians will expect you to be close to where you were when they attacked you last." He answered. "When they find you gone they will pick up your trail and follow it. I am going to take my troopers and set up an ambush if you can spare a man to show where you were."

"I got the best man for you," I told him, "A K our Sioux drover. He will lead you to the exact spot."

"A Sioux?" He questioned with a puzzled look.

"Yes he's been with us for seventeen years and has saved our tails many times."

"OK Brad, get him to me and we will get moving. Get your wagons in a cluster and give a rifle to anyone that can shoot and put them in the wagons. I am sure some will get by us and they will attack the wagons first."

"Alright Captain Munson," I said with a smile, "I'll get right on it. Thanks for your help." He gave me a big smile and a salute. I got A K to get with him and the Cavalry moved south. John had our meal ready and all were happy to eat. The Roberts family joined us and Amber was happy to talk to some ladies' for a change. They got some food on their plates and sat together and started talking away. Lee Tingy told me as he was driving the wagon for Mrs. Dorothy Roberts and her Mom Mrs. Hartman they told him they were Mormons going to Salt Lake City to see the new Mormon Temple built there and was dedicated this June. The Mormons were persecuted and bullied around by a lot of other settlers because of their religion and their beliefs. They were hoping to get into a community of other Mormons and start their own ranch or farm. A lot of the Mormon settlements were destroyed by those who mistrusted them because of their different religious ways. They believed in Jesus Christ very deeply. They seemed like good honest hard working people and very helpful and friendly.

Dad told everyone to get some rest and be ready at the break of dawn. We got the wagons together so we could defend ourselves if attacked. I was hoping we wouldn't be but Captain Munson said some might get through his defense. Knowing Indians from the years I fought them I knew that he was right and it was a very good possibility. I got Amber into a wagon. She didn't want be in the wagon, but I insisted for her safety. I made sure she had her rifle and wished her a good night. She gave me a kiss and told me to be careful. I went back to the fire as I rolled me a smoke and sat with Cookie John and he shared a good belt of whiskey with me and some of the men. We talked awhile, mostly about Indians and past encounters we had with them through the years. I grabbed my tarp and blankets and settled next to the fire and tried to get some sleep. It had been a long day.

Chapter Twenty Five

 At the break of day the Indians, about a hundred strong, rushed in for their attack and found us gone. A quick look at the ground and they found our trail heading north. They turned their ponies and raced ahead at a hard run. Just as they topped a rise they ran right into the ambush of troopers set up by Captain Munson. I was standing by the fire, drinking coffee, rifle in hand when I heard the troopers open fire. We all ran for cover around and under the wagons. It has been a long time since I've heard that much gunfire.
 The Captain swung his sword down to give them the command to fire. A large number of warriors hit the ground. The rest pulled their horses back in full retreat. They were caught completely by surprise. Sly Wolf ordered his braves to split up and to go around and hit them from both sides at once. That didn't work either as Captain Munson had troopers stationed in a line on both sides in case the warriors would in fact do just that. Again a lot of braves hit the ground. They had to pull back again. In just a few moments the Indians lost almost half their entire force. Sly Wolf saw A K with the troopers and rode out in front of them with a white rag tied to his rifle and called his name.
 He said in Sioux language.

"Akecheta Otaktay! You are a traitor and a disgrace to your own kind and I
challenge you to a fight to the death with knives. Unless you are a coward."

"You don't have to go out there," Captain Munson told A K, "We have all in control and will defeat them."

"You do not understand," A K answered, "I must do this, that's how we are born. I must go." A K handed his rifle and pistol belt to the Captain and rode out to meet Sly Wolf. They sat forty yards apart on their horses.

"I will kill you." Sly Wolf shouted and charged his horse at A K. A K edged his horse at a full run to meet him. Their horses collided with a loud thud and Sly Wolf was knocked off his stead and A K jumped off his mount knife in hand. Sly Wolf lunged up and took a swing at A K with his blade. A K stepped back to avoid his knife and then rushed quickly at him swinging his blade. Sly Wolf jumped forward and with his foot kicked A K to the ground. He then tried to pounce on A K and stab him. A K rolled over and sprang to his feet. As he did Sly Wolf swung his blade at A K's chest giving him a deep slash. A K staggered.

"Even a squaw gets lucky." He said to Sly Wolf.

"Even a squaw can kill a coward." Sly Wolf replied and lunged at A K again. As he did A K grabbed his arm and stuck his knife deep into Sly Wolfs mid section. Sly Wolf dropped to his knees holding his wound. He was bleeding badly. A K knocked him on his back and held his blade to Sly Wolf's throat. But he hesitated and got to his feet.

"It's over," A K told him. "We are not the warriors we once were, and we are no better than the white man now. You're badly wounded, but maybe you will live if you get help quickly."

Sly Wolf grabbed his knife and shouted,

"You did not kill me. I will not let you." He them took his knife and drove it deep into his chest and his eyes closed.

"Farewell my brother," A K said, "You fought brave and well. May the Great Spirit provide you many buffalo to hunt and Squaws for you lodge." A K turned and walked away holding his bandana over his wound.

"Get that man some help quickly," the Captain ordered, "He's cut deep." A couple of troopers ran to him to see what they could do. The rest of the braves picked up Sly Wolf and carried him away.

"We will meet again." One of the braves hollered. A K raised his hand in the air in reply.

"We got to get him back to the fort," Captain Munson ordered, "He needs attention, he's bleeding badly." A K mounted his horse and one of the troopers took the reins to lead him.

When they got back to the wagons Sister Dorothy Roberts and the other women came to help the wounded men.

"I got twelve wounded and A K is badly cut," Munson said and pointed to his sergeant, "Run to the fort and get the Doc, quickly. Some of you men get the worst of the wounded over by the wagons so the Doctor and lady's can care for them. The rest of you set up a perimeter for defense just in case."

Sister Roberts looked at A K's wound and told Sister Rebecca to get her sewing box.

"This man needs stitches." She said.

A K looked at her. "Stitches," he said, "You going to fix me like a croaker sack?" Miss Roberts smiled and started washing A K's wound. Rebecca and Ce Ce brought the sewing basket and Miss Roberts started to stitch A K's wound.

When the Doctor got there I recognized him. It was David Saint. He was the doctor at Fort Scott when I was in the Cavalry.

"Hi Doc," I said, "How have you been?'

"Hello Brad, I'm doing well, good to see you again. The army and the Indians keep me busy. Always someone to patch up around here these days. Maybe some day we will stop trying to kill each other."

Dr Saint saved my life when I had a serious chest wound I received during an Indian raid on us in Kansas. He's one of the best. He went to work on the wounded troopers with

some help from the lady's in our camp. He looked at A K's
wound and told Sister Roberts,
"You did a great job fixing him up. Nothing left for me to
do. I couldn't have done better myself."
"Thank you Doctor, "Miss Roberts replied, "I worked for a
doctor back east for a couple of years. I used a double
strand of silk thread, it won't stick to the wound and it's
less of a chance for infection."
"Well you did well young lady. Do you want to help me
with the others?"
"Yes I'd be glad to help sir."
Dad came to me and said he was going to pick out a young
fat steer from the herd and have John cook it to feed the
men and ladies in camp.
"I am going to tell Captain Munson we will feed the
troopers that helped us," Dad told me, "I think they will
enjoy some good roast beef. Besides we are making good
time and we only got about two hundred miles or so to St.
Louis. A day off to rest would do our men some good. Brad
you need to go into town and to see if your Mother sent us
any telly's.
I had told my Dad that I had sent telegrams to Mom and
Patti when I was in Batesville and for them to send their
reply to us in West Plains and I would pick them up there
and answer them. Amber decided to stay and help around
camp to treat the wounded troopers. Thankfully none of

them were very seriously wounded and they would recover in a short time. Captain Munson said he didn't think the Indians would attack us again as they lost many warriors and we were so close to the Fort. He also said he was going to take a couple of Indian scouts and fifty or more troopers and track them to their camp. Once there he was going to have the scouts tell them if they caused anymore trouble they would quickly pay the price of retaliation. Hopefully we won't have anymore Indian trouble on the rest of our drive. I asked Rick and Harry if they wanted to go into town with me but they didn't seem to want to go. Lee Tingy and Don Volsch said they would like to go into town so we mounted up and rode in.

West Plains was a clean looking community and busy with freight wagons. There were a few cowhands and several prospectors, a couple of Hotels and a couple of Saloons. I noticed a man walking our way with a badge on his vest.

"Howdy boys," He said waving his hand at us, "Just passin' through?"

"Yes sir," I replied, "We are with the cattle drive outside of town and I have to check to see if I have any telegrams. Nice town you have here."

"Yes and I try to keep that way," He answered, "Weren't always that way till I came here. Just don't cause any trouble and if you run into a fuss let me handle it. Don't want no gun play here. The post office is the building with the flag in front." I thanked him and told him we weren't looking for any trouble either. I rode to the post office and Don and Lee said to meet them in the saloon across the street and have a drink after I was done. I dismounted and went inside. There a man sorting mail behind a counter.

"Hello," I said, "Do you have any telegrams for Brad Lassiter?"

Think I do," He answered, "Two of 'em I believe, let me look. Yup, here they are fella'. You Lassiter?"

"Yes sir I am from Lufkin Texas."

"Long way from yer home ain't ya son?" He asked as he handed the papers to me. "If 'in you weren't Lassiter I'd have ta get ya to sign for 'em."

"Thank you sir, here's four bits for your care and trouble."

"Don't need to do that me boy," He said with a smile, "But that's most fine of ya! It'll buy me a drink 'er two after work. Much obliged young man, very much indeed." I tipped my hat as I left and walked over to the saloon to meet Don and Lee. There were a few customers there playing cards and a few sitting at tables having a drink and talking. Don bought me a drink and I took it to a table so I could read the telly's. The first was from Miss Fogt and she said all was going well, store sales were up and Rick and Max bought two more big horses. She said not to worry, everything was fine and to hurry home.

The second was from my Mom and she said Rhett Berman came over with some men and did some fix up work around the ranch. She also said Rhett brought about thirty head of cattle with the Lassiter brand on them. He said he didn't know how they got into the Berman herd and brought them over to her. I guess they just wondered over there. Boy dad will get a kick out of that. I rolled me a smoke and enjoyed my drink. After buying a round for the three of us I went back to the post office and sent a reply back to both Mom and Patti telling them the next time I would check for telegrams would be in the town of Sullivan Missouri.

We got back to our camp and Cookie John had the steer over the fire, this was going to be and good dinner. The wounded troopers were doing well and the others were all around our fire and wagons every body was talking to somebody.

Ce Ce went to sit next to A K.

"How are you doing A K?" She asked. "Are you going to be O K?"

"Just fine young lady," He replied, "Miss Roberts patched me up real good and tight. Just a little sore but I will be in the saddle in a day or so."

"Don't over do your self A K, take time to heal." Ce Ce told him. He nodded his head and smiled.

"A K, I didn't get a chance to thank you for saving me and returning me to my Grandmom. I wish to thank you very much. It was wonderful of you to put your neck on the line for me."

"I was glad I could pull it off young lady. Happy to do it."

"I just have to ask you A K, how do you feel about fighting your own kind? Doesn't it bother you?"

A K looked at her and answered.

"Miss, we are no better than the white man now. The white man took all away from us when they came west. Stole our land, killed off all our food and raided our villages. They killed us and didn't feel guilty at all. A herd of buffalo could take a day to pass by, and now they are gone. Then yellow metal was found and they took even more land and killed even more of us."

"That's such a shame." Ce Ce said.

"Yes it is but now the Indian does as the whites have taught them. Steal and kill, and in turn the whites take revenge and it goes on back and forth. I came to the Lassiter Ranch in 1876 when Charlie Lassiter saved my life. I will stay and work for him till I die. I owe my life to him. But that's another story." Ce Ce gave him a hug and went back to sit with her Grandmom.

Chapter Twenty Six

 Just as it was getting dark a wagon train of about twelve
wagons came rolling in out side of the fort. John was
finishing up the meal preparations and getting set up to feed
everyone. I looked up and here came Miss Leslie
Montgomery.
"Hi me darlings," She said to Amber and I, "How's me
darlings doing? Is all well?" We told her about the Indian
raids and how the cavalry and the Roberts family helped us
in our time of need.
"Well me darlings, how about some whiskey to help
smooth things down a little?" Miss Leslie asked.
"That sounds really good," I replied, "But we got a lot of
people here."
"Not to worry young man," She said with a smile, "I got
two wagons full of whisky brandy and wine. I think I can
share some with you folks."
 So that's what business she had in Willow Springs, I
thought to myself. So she's not just in the hotel business,
she's selling whiskey too! What a character this lady is.
She walked back to one of her wagons and she and a young
lady came back each carrying a case.
"This is Leah Maxey," She said, "Leah, meet Brad and
Amber Lassiter." Amber shook her hand and I tipped my
hat. "She helps me run the hotel business. I am opening a

Hotel in Willow Springs and Leah will be operating it for me. Tell the men to take a shot or two and pass 'em around. Leah take some bottles to the wounded troopers. That'll help 'em feel better." She had a big grin on her face. The young lady carried some bottles to the wounded troopers and passed them out. Them she returned and said.

"Miss Leslie told me all about your wedding. She said it was a great time you all had."

"It sure was," I told her, "Miss Leslie and Jessica took real good care of us. It was first class all the way. We had a wonderful stay and I will never forget it."

Cookie John had the steer roasted and a couple of large pots of beans and rice.

"Dig in and get it," He shouted," Ladies and young 'ins first." He started carving the meat from the steer and dished it out. The ladies and Bill's children made plates for the wounded troopers and handed them out then came back to get theirs. We had a couple of shots of whiskey and got in line for a fine meal. After eating Dad and Steve sat with Amber and I. I rolled a smoke, we drank coffee and talked among ourselves. It was nice to see Dad relax for a change. The ladies helped Cookie clean up and pack things away while talking lady things I guess. John enjoyed the lady's and joked with them as they worked. They were a big help to him. John cut the rest of the meat from the steer and salted it to put away for another time.

"Well son we hit the trail tomorrow," Dad said, "Got about eighteen days to go as I got it figured."

I smiled and replied. "We've made good time Dad. I'm hoping we don't run into anymore trouble. Not that's it been so big that we couldn't handle it. But if it wasn't for the Cav this last go round could have been much different."

"I'd say all an all we had a good run," Steve added, "Like you said a little trouble here and there but it was manageable." We talked for a while longer and Bill Roberts came over to see us. He told us that he and his folks would be leaving and heading west in the morning. Dad told him to wait a minute and he would be right back. He returned in a minute with a rifle in hand.

"Here young man," Dad said, "Here's a Henry 44-40 and fifty rounds of ammo. We got it from one of the Indians we took down. It will give you a good gun to protect you and your family."

"Thank you Mr. Lassiter," Bill replied, "I will keep this rifle and pass it on to my son Cameron. Thank you very much indeed sir."

Dad patted him on the back and continued. "I want to thank you for helping to save us and the herd. You're a fine young man. If you ever get to Texas come see us at the ranch. It's just outside Lufkin."

"I will for sure if I come that way sir. And thank you again." He shook Dad's hand and tipped his hat at the rest of us. Captain Munson came to us and said he was heading out in the morning to find that Indian camp and put the fear of Hell into them. He shook dads hand and then asked me, "Brad that fellow with the brown flat rimed hat, what's his name?"

"Matt Barnes," I answered, "Why do you ask?"

"I got a poster from the U. S. Marshalls office and it looks a lot like him except the poster shows him with a mustache. Say's Chuck Shoemaker, wanted for questioning in several states for gun fights ending in death."

"I've had others ask about him, "Captain, "But he seems like a straight forward guy. Keeps to himself a lot but he's a good cowhand."

"I didn't think you would have him if he wasn't," Captain Munson said, "Anyway hope all goes well for you on the rest of the drive. Good to see you again Brad. Take care pal."

"You too Chuck," I answered, "Be careful and ride safe, good to see you also!" We shook hands and he tipped his hat to Amber and went back to his men.

"Good night Brad, Amber, see ya in the morn. Gotta get some sleep." Dad told us and wished the men around us a good sleep also.

Meanwhile Mr. Witt walked over to Miss Harris's and Ce Ce's wagon. They saw him coming and stood up to meet him.

"Miss Harris I'd like to ask you something if I may." He said

"Yes Richard, what is it?"

"Miss Harris if you'll follow us to St. Louis and when we get all settled with the herd I'd like to drive you and your wagon to Oklahoma and start us a farm or a ranch." He said with his hat in his hands nervously. "That is if 'in you'll have me ma'am."

"Richard I certainly would love to have you. I have been waiting for you a long time"

"Well ma'am as I said I got caught up in the west, but I thought of you a lot. I should have writ-in' you but I didn't. I figured you done got hitched and wouldn't need me none a tall."

"Well Mr. Witt I didn't get hitched as you say and we finally got together and I am pleased to have you for my man." Richard stepped to Miss Harris and gave her a kiss and they hugged.

"Well ma'am, good night and yall get some sleep and I'll be seeing you in the morn."

"Good night Richard see you in the morning." She turned and gave Ce Ce a hug. I could tell she was very happy! We all turned in for the night. Tomorrow it was back to work.

Chapter Twenty Seven

Morning seemed to come awfully quick. I got up and got coffee for Amber and I got ready for the morning meal. I'd noticed the air was getting more of a chill to it as we've moved north. We got near the fire to warm up and wait for Cookie to tell us to come and get it. Joe Parmer walked over to where we were sitting and announced; "The strangers Harry and Rick appear to have left."
"When did they leave?" I asked.
"Just before day break," A K told us, "They paid Steve Lowery a twenty dollar gold piece to pull their horses shoes and put them in their saddle bags."
"Did they take anything?" I asked.
"Nope not a thing," A K replied, "They rode over to the camp of the Missoura Indians and talked to one of the tribe. They handed him something, shook his hand and rode on."
"Strange pair of men," I said, "Did Matt go with them?"
"Nope, he's here having coffee over by the wagons." Joe answered.
They said they would ride with us for a while to help us and they did. Don't know why they didn't say good bye. They were a great help though. I wonder about their past. But all and all it was good to have their help. Maybe Matt might know more. I'll have to ask him.

The Roberts wagons and the group Miss Montgomery was with pulled out early after saying goodbye. I hoped they all have a safe journey. John served a breakfast of bacon, scrambled eggs and biscuits', it was a good meal. Amber and I got our mounts for the day and saddled them up.

"It's chilly this morning, Brad. Glad I got this jacket, gonna' need it for a while till the sun gets higher."

"Your right my dear it is nippy this morning," I answered, "I think it's gonna be like this for the rest of the drive. Colder nights are coming!"

"RO-L-L-L-L 'EM OUT," Arnie ordered and we started moving the cattle northward. The buffalo was still up front of the herd acting as he was the boss. I just cannot get over that. He was pretty docile for an animal out of the wild. Didn't give the men any trouble unless they got to close, but at that all he did was snort and shake his head at them. Strange indeed. I don't know what we are going to do with him when we get to St. Louis.

About an hour out we could see four riders coming up behind us. They stopped and talked to Lee Tingy who was at the end of the herd. Lee pointed north and they road by me and went toward the front of the herd to where Dad and Arnie were. I followed them just in case. I had no idea who they were or what they were up too! They looked real serious. When they got to where dad was one said, "Who's the Boss here?"

Dad answered. "That's me, what's your business?"

"I'm Edward Buist, Federal Marshal. These are my deputies, Milt Martin, Kevin Smith and Tom Baboni. Need to see all your men."

"What's the problem?" Dad replied. "I got men all around the herd. Can't just call them in. Gotta' keep the cattle strung out."

."The problem is I got warrants for two men and I believe who we are lookin' for is with your group." He commanded.

"We'll have to go around to see them all." Dad told the Marshal.

"OK let ride out and see 'em." The Marshall answered.

Dad agreed and they started around the herd. The other deputies split up and went the other way. I wondered if it was the strangers Rick and Harry they were after or maybe Matt. I had no idea. They went from man to man but paid no attention to the Mexican Vaqueros at all. After seeing all the men they gathered back together.

"Well?" Marshal Buist asked his men, "What did ya see?"

"Don't appear to be here sir." One deputy answered. "No sign of 'em 'a tall."

Marshal Buist turned to ad.

"Did you have a couple of men join you a couple of weeks back?"

"I've seen strangers come and pass." Dad said. "Always meeting some here and there on the trail. Mostly miners or trappers, who are these guys?"

The Marshal turned to one of his men and asked for the papers. He unrolled them and handed them to my dad. Dads eyes went wide open.

"Are you kidding," he asked, "I don't know anyone by the name of Harry Longbaugh or Robert Parker by name. Gotta' picture?"

"Maybe you'd know them by their alias," The Marshal answered. "Butch Cassidy and the Sundance Kid. We picked up their trail and it led to your cattle drive. Then we got attacked by a rogue band of Comanche's, wounded one of my deputies and killed our Indian scout. That put us behind a bit."

"Butch and Sundance," Arnie said, "What are they doing in these parts?"

"Running from the law. Something they do a lot of these days seems like." Marshal Buist answered, "So dang hard to get 'em cornered. Those boys are like hunt' in ghosts' or Apaches."

"Well Marshal Buist, ifin' we'd seen 'em I'm sure they wouldn't had told us who they were, that's for sure."

"Guess so Mr. Lassiter, sorry to take up your time. Come on boys we gotta back track and look for some sign. Thanks again. Oh by the way Mr. Lassiter, what's the name of that guy you have riding with you with the flat brimmed brown hat and black leather jacket?"

"Matt Barnes, his name," Dad replied, "Good cow hand."

"Looks familiar," Marshal Buist said, "Just can't place it though. Oh well gotta go." He circled his horse and he and his men rode south. I asked my dad why he didn't tell the Marshall about the strangers Rick and Harry. He said they were a big help to us and he wasn't about to sell them out. They would have to handle it on their own and if that's who they were sooner or later they would get caught.

Boy I thought, I'll bet that's who those strangers were. Butch and Sundance and I got a feeling Matt knew who they were. He didn't say anything to us about them, but again, what if he in fact was Chuck Shoemaker the gunslinger? If that's the case they most likely did know each other. But I got an idea in my head that just might answer the question.

The sun was warming it up nicely and I was glad as I didn't have a cold weather jacket on. We were a few miles south of Willow Springs making good time. The cool weather made the cattle a little frisky and we were slowing them down more than pushing them. Dad said we would pass the town on the west side. He asked me to run into town to get some things for Cookie John as we used up some items feeding the men and the troopers. He gave me a list and some money and told me when the herd got to

Mountain Grove he would head north east toward the town of Salem. I wouldn't be too long in town so it would be easy for me to catch up to them quickly. I waited for the noon break so I could get with the men to see if they needed anything. Most wanted fixins' for smokes, a few wanted new socks and Amber said she would like some licorice I thought this would be a good time to try my plan on Matt so I asked him to go with me.

I went to Carlen and had him set up two pack horses for me. I then grabbed some coffee and ate some beef stew and biscuits. Then Matt and I mounted up to ride into town. As we were riding we talked some small talk and I avoided talking about Rick and Harry like it didn't happen. I started to ease back and let Matt ride in front of me. It wasn't long we could see Willow Springs ahead. Not a very big town kinda' small in fact. Matt was about twenty yards ahead when I decided to make my move.

I hollered, "CHUCK" In load voice. In a flash he turned pistol in hand. I put my hands up to show I wasn't making a move for my pistol. He looked at me with a blank look on his face.

"I guess the cat's out of the bag." I said to him. "Wanta' talk?"

"Yea I guess so." He answered. "You want me to pack out Brad?"

217

"No, all is OK with me," I told him, "I just had to find out sooner or later. Are you Chuck Shoemaker?"

"Ya Brad, that's me. I was hoping that I wouldn't be found out. So what you want to know?"

"I've been thinking for a while that's who you were, but I just had to find out for myself."

"I've been trying to get out of the gun fighting trade for quite awhile but it just keeps following me and I want to get away from it."

"Back at the raid in the canyon one of Bermans men knew you didn't he?"

Ya, but I tried to ignore him."

"Well he was right you're as fast as lighting."

"One of these days somebody's gonna' be quicker Brad, and I'm trying to change. I want a place of my own and settle with a good woman, but someone always shows up that knows me. I wish I could shed it. I never hunted a man or got paid to kill a man; I never drew unless it was self defense or helping a friend
in need. But being fast always draws hot shots looking to beat me."

"Matt you're trying to put your past behind you and you're trying to get your life together. You're a good cow hand and your secret is safe with me Matt. I won't say anything to no one. You deserve a chance"

"Thanks Brad, that means a lot to me. I consider you a friend. A good one too."

"By the way Matt did you know those two, Rick and Harry?"

"Yes we've ran into each other from time to time in the past. I knew they were dodging a posse and I didn't want to sell them out. They would have done the same for me."

"OK Matt lets get those supplies and we won't talk about Chuck Shoemaker anymore unless you want to!"

Chapter Twenty Eight

We rode into Willow Springs and tied up in front of a store that said, Whole Goods and Supplies. I walked in and a short stocky man greeted us.

"Howdy boy's can I help ya?"

"I need these items for our drive." I showed him the list. "Can you fill this for me?" He looked it over.

"Sure can," he said, "Cash only though. Been stuck by strangers too many times. No offense to ya', just gotta' cover myself. Supplies been hard to come by lately."

"No problem, cash I got. Don't blame you at all. How long will it take?"

"Leave your pack horses tied to the rail; I'll load 'em up, be done in no time."

"OK," I said, "We'll step to the saloon have us a shot and some coffee." He waved his hand with a thumb's up and started pulling items.

The saloon had a few cow hands and miners sitting around at the tables, some playing cards others just sitting and talking. It appeared to be the biggest building in town. Nothing fancy but clean and orderly.

"Howdy boys, what's you pleasure?" A heavy set red faced man in his fifty's behind the bar asked. "Got cold beer today or whisky today."

"I'll have a shot, how about you Matt?"

"Sounds good to me Brad." Matt said and threw two silver dollars on the bar.

"Want some ice in 'em?" The bartender said. "We got ice today too!"

"That sounds good sir." I replied, "Don't see ice often, that's a treat."

"Got an ole boy brings it in from the mountains. He cuts it in the winter and saves it in a cave somewhere up there a bouts'. Where you boys from? Ain't seen ya afore'."

"We're from Lufkin Texas, pushing cattle to St. Louis. Just in town for supplies and thought we'd have us a drink." I told him. When I said that two cowboys that looked to be in their late twenties got up from their table and walked to the bar.

"St. Louis?" The bartender asked. "Dint' think nobody went that far anymore. How the hell did you get this far? Most areas closed now days."

"It's been a little tricky," I told him, "But so far so good."

"Lufkin?" One of the two at the bar asked. "What ranch ya from?" The bartender leaned to me and whispered. "Careful son, that's Travis Dice and Travis Barrow. Them boys are trouble." I nodded at him and tapped Matt to be alert but I could see his instinct was already working as he turned to face them.

"Lassiter ranch near Lufkin," I answered, "Why you asking?"

"I got twin brothers working for the Berman Ranch near Lufkin. They got beat up bad by a couple a Lassiter boys and thrown in jail a couple of months back. Is Brad Lassiter with your drive?"

"Well yes he is young man," I replied, "Your look' in at him."

"Well I think I want to settle things up for the Dice family." He said.

"They were the ones that started the fuss and got what they deserved." I told him.

"How about you take us on Mr. Brad. Fists or guns? What it'll be, cowman."

"I don't think you'll want do guns Mr. Dice," I told him, "Better use your fists."

"I'm pretty quick fella'." He said, "Pretty quick indeed."

"You as fast as Chuck Shoemaker?" With that Chuck looked at me with surprise and I winked at him.

"I would like to meet Shoemaker," He replied, "Is that him with you or is he outside?"

"No this is Matt Barnes," I told him, "He killed Chuck Shoemaker a couple months back outside of Crocket Texas." With that everyone in the bar we're looking at us.

"You can't be that quick, even Bill Hickok wouldn't have tried Shoemaker, he was fast, shoot him in the back did ya?"

"No he did it fair 'en square out of self defense." I told him.

"OK boys," the bartender said, "Let's have no fightin' or shootin' in here. I don't want nuttin' broke up."

"I don't want to cause you any trouble Mr. Bartender. Somebody get the sheriff in here." I said to the others in the bar.

"Sheriff's home with a broke leg, ain't no help here." Someone answered.

"I don't want no trouble Dice. Your brothers attacked me and Matt helped me give it to 'em. Now back down."

"Let's get outside Lassiter, we'll see how tough you are." I looked at Chuck and he nodded his head.

"Suits me." He said. "Lets get at it."

By this time the bartender had a shot gun on the bar. "OK boys," he ordered, "Leave your gun belts on the bar."

"I ain't takin' my gun off for nobody." Travis Barrow replied. With that the bartender cocked his double barrel and said, "Take 'em off or I'll mess up my own bar."

"Let's just forget it," Travis Dice said, "Just let it go. There will be another time. Come on partner." He said to Barrow and the two of them backed out the door. The bartender said to us. "Better keep an eye out boys, I don't trust them at all."

We thanked him and paid for our drinks and stepped to the door and looked out. Barrow and Dice were walking down the street to the livery stable. I looked at Chuck and said. "Well Matt Barnes, Shoemaker is dead and it won't take long for the word to spread. From now on you're Matt Barnes. Maybe you'll finally find peace."

"I hope so Brad, just hope some hot shot doesn't look me up to prove something."

We went to the store got some smoke fixin's for the men Cookies supplies and Amber's candy. We paid the store keeper and mounted up. We rode out of town and started looking for the trail left by the drive. We found the trail and started after the herd. About a half hour out my horse stopped with his ears pointed forward snorted and whinnied.

"Hold up cowboys," someone shouted, "Just hold it right there." Travis Barrow stepped out of some brush with rifle in hand. "Just get down and keep yer hands away from yer guns." He said pointing his rifle. As we got off our mounts Travis Dice stepped out next with a grin on his face.

"O K Mr. Barnes,' He said, "lets see if you got what it takes. Barrow you keep yer eye on Mr. Brad."

"I don't think you want to do this," I said, "Don't be a fool and leave us ride on."

"Not without settling this. Now get out 'ta way." He stood there with his hand over his gun. Matt stepped toward him not stopping. Travis Dice was getting nervous and took a step back but Matt just kept walking to him. Dice went for his gun. A shot rang out and Travis Dice dropped backward with his pistol in hand. At that Barrow lifted his rifle to shoot Matt and I dropped him. Both were hit dead center in the chest. They were dead.

"Damn," Matt said, "I was hoping it wouldn't have come to this. Does it ever end?"

"I hope it will now Matt, I hope so."

Chapter Twenty Nine

Matt and I put Dice and Barrow over their horses and tied them securely knowing the horses would find their way back home. We caught up to the herd just east of Mountain Grove Missouri. I took the pack horses to Cookie John and helped him unload them. Amber rode up and I gave her the licorice candy she asked for. That made her very happy. The men got the items I picked up for them and paid me. They were happy to get the fixins' for smoking as most had just used the last they had. Dad said we were making real good time and we would come to the town of Salem in a couple of days. After Salem we would be about ten days out from St. Louis. The weather was good and clear. There was a chill in the air and the nights were getting cooler and I was happy to snuggle with Amber to keep warm. We were surrounded by mountains on both sides but it keeps the cattle together. The down side was it got dark early when the sun went over the mountainside. Cookie John had shot a couple of deer for camp meat. He chopped up the deer liver and added it to our gravy for breakfast. That was real tasty. We were eating very well on this drive.

We keep up the pace but not too hard as to cause the cattle to lose weight. There was plenty of good grass for the herd to feed on when we stopped though. We were getting close to town of Salem when a rider came up on a nice Dun horse. Arnie rode to meet him.

"Can I help ya?" Arnie asked.

"Who's the boss on this drive?" The rider asked. "I'm Sheriff Alex Schuring from Salem. You gotta' stop here and turn around and find another way."

"Turn around," Arnie replied, "there ain't no other way."

"On the north side of town it's all farm land and the farmers don't need their crops torn up. On the south side the town is up against the mountains and you can't get through there and you ain't gonna' go through town. That's what I'm here to tell ya!"

Arnie turned to Joe Parmer.

"Get Charlie up here." He said.

Joe went and got Dad and he and the sheriff talked for several minutes trying to explain that to turn around would put us behind by days and a hundred miles out of our way. Sheriff Alex wouldn't back down and told Dad he had no choice. The talk got pretty well heated but the sheriff wouldn't change his mind. He told Dad if he went through town he would arrest him.

Dad cussed and threw his hat on the ground.

"OK boys," He said, "Hold 'em up." The sheriff bid him good day and rode back to town. I asked Dad what we were going to do. It will put us behind in a big way.

"Just tell Cookie to start the evening meal." He answered. "Let me think this out. I gotta' do some figuring."
After eating his meal Dad told the men to get some rest and he and Arnie walked off to talk. Amber came to me and we went to eat our meal with Miss Harris, Ce Ce and Mr. Witt. Miss Harris was very excited about her up coming marriage to Mr. Witt and that's about all we talked of. I rolled a smoke and asked Richard if he wanted to go to Cookies wagon with me and have a shot of good whiskey while the ladies gabbed about Miss Harris's plans. He seemed real happy to talk about something other than the big event. We talked a while with Cookie John and a few of the men hanging around the fire and I passed around the bottle that Miss Montgomery gave me. That was some good whiskey. It even had a label on it that said, Forbes Pure Rye, Philadelphia, Pa. We sat and talked for a while stoking the fire and helped John clean up the pots and cooking gear to be ready for breakfast. Then we decided to get some rest and then Dad and Arnie came walking up.
"Cookie," he said, "Get your gear packed and mules hitched. Mr. Witt, hook up Miss Harris's oxen to the wagon, Steve get your team hooked up and Yall get ready to move out."
"Where are we going Dad?"
"I'll let ya know shortly son. Arnie, you see to the men."
"OK Boss," He answered, "I'll get 'em ready."

All of a sudden the camp was busy and everyone was doing something to get ready to go somewhere but only Arnie and Dad knew where that was. About ten thirty Dad told John to move the wagons east through Salem and don't be slack about it and move as quick as they could. With that all the wagons moved out heading for the town of Salem. I just couldn't think of where Dad was going to move the herd. All the men were in the saddle and gathering up the herd. A lot of them were asking where we were heading, but no one knew. Just before midnight Trent Arthur came riding in from the direction of town and talked with Dad.

"Get the lead steers in front and let's Move 'em east." Dad shouted. "Don't let no grass grow below their feet. Move 'em fast."

I can't believe what I just heard him say. We can't run thirty eight hundred head of cattle through that small town at a stampede pace. That'll really do some damage. Dad motioned me forward and he rode to the front of the drive. When we got there no one was in the street and those that were still up were in the saloon. The cattle came down the street at a good pace with our drovers hooping and hollering knocking down signs, lampposts and ripping down pillars that held the porch roof's and tearing up the wooden side walks. What a mess this was going to be and

how did Dad think he was going to get away with it. In the older days we
would often drive through a town but at a slow pace as not to wreck much of
anything. But those days are over and town's people were tired of cowhand drinking and shootin' things up. All but the saloon keepers that is, as they liked the cowhand's money and had so many ways to get it. Matt Yeaton, Lee Tingy and Don Volsch brought up the end of the herd and as they rode through someone took some shots at them from an alley. None of them were hit but Matt's horse went down hit in the leg. Matt pulled the bridle and his saddle as Lee and Don rode back shooting in all directions to get him. Don took Matt's gear. Matt shot his horse to put it out of it's misery before he jumped up behind Lee and they rode after the herd.

As we cleared the town we slowed down the herd and continued through the night heading in a northerly direction going through a pass in the mountains heading toward the town of Rolla. We drove the cattle until almost day break and Arnie put the word out for Cookie to make breakfast and for the men to get some much need rest. I know I was worn out and ready for a break. Amber brought me a cup of coffee and we waited for Cookie John to finish the meal. Miss Harris and Ce Ce stepped in to give John a hand. A lot of the drovers were sitting next to a fire they had built to warm themselves. It was a cool morning and over cast with clouds in the sky. Dad came riding up to us.

"Eat your meal and get some rest," He said, "We'll hold the herd here and move 'em at noon. Eat hardy as we ain't stopping for a nooner'." Dad looked tired. In fact we all looked tired. We ate a big breakfast and I was ready for a nap. Amber got a couple of blankets and we snuggled up by the fire. My belly was full and I fell to sleep immediately.

At noon time the trail boss Arnie shouted, "Move 'em out boys times a waste 'in." Lets get these doggies stepping." We all started throwing saddles on our horses to get pushing the herd. I looked down the trail and saw five riders coming at a good pace. I hollered to my brother Steve and pointed them out. Steve pulled his rifle and he and Howard Brandon and I rode to meet them. As we got closer I recognized Sheriff Alex Schuring was one of them. I knew this was going to be trouble. I told Howard to get my Dad.

"Where's the boss man?" Sheriff Alex demanded. "Get 'em over here and now."

"I sent for him Sheriff," I told him, "he's coming."

Dad came riding up and the Sheriff jumped on his tail. "I told you not to drive through town fella'. What part of that did you not understand? I got a warrant here for your arrest. You did a lot of damage." The sheriff pointed at his men. "This is Wilburn Baker, the town's mayor. This here is

Bucky Bishop he is the town lawyer and they are pressing charges."

"How much damage did it do sheriff?" Dad asked.

"Couldn't have done too much damage. We went through as fast as we could." Dad said with a grin on his face.

"Ain't funny atall', wipe yer' smile off yer face! You tore down lamp posts, porch pillars, signs and most of the side walks are wrecked." The sheriff said angrily.

"Lady's don't like walking in the mud and dirt."

'We will be seeking restitution," Lawyer Bishop said, "You ran up quite a bill of damage. The town looks like a Nor-Easter went through it. Going to take a lot of men and money to straighten things out in town. And you are not going anywhere until it's paid for. If you decide to run we will have the U.S. Marshall bring you back for a trial."

"Well how about if I pay for it?" Dad asked. "How much can it be?"

" The bill to fix all the damage is six hundred and fifty dollars," Mayor Baker said, "You can pay it now or wait in jail until you can have it delivered."

"Well boys lets talk this over," Dad said and got off his horse, "I'm sure we can work this out."

"Better be good." Lawyer Bishop said. They all got off their horses and walked aside

"I'll write a letter for you to telegraph my bank and transfer the money to your town." Dad told him. "I'll get two of my men to witness it. That ought to do it."

The Sherriff, the Mayor and the Lawyer huddled together for a few minutes and talked. They nodded their heads and walked back to my Dad.

"OK Mr. Lassiter," Lawyer Bishop announced, "If something goes wrong we will have the Marshall haul you back. I will also need twenty five dollars for my legal expertise."

"Twenty five dollars?" Dad replied, "You lawyers are as bad as highway men. That's outrageous. Just to send a telegram? You dang layers use the law to rob people."

"Keep it up Mr. Lassiter and I'll charge you an additional twenty five for slandering my character in public."

"Slander? Just because I said a skunk smelled bad?" Dad answered.

"Take it or leave it," Bishop said, "Or you can sit in jail until we get the money."

"OK, OK," Dad replied, "let's get it done so I can move this herd." Dad got a paper and wrote out his letter to the bank and had me and Steve witness it. He shook the Sheriffs and the Mayors hands and tipped his hat to Bucky Bishop. Then dad climbed into his saddle. "O K boys let's get 'em moving." He ordered and rode to toward the front of the herd. All in all I think we got off pretty well, dad told me later. He had already figured on that happening and he knew he was going to have to pay for the damage to the town, but in the long run it was cheaper than going more than seventy five miles out of our way.

The pass through the mountains was narrow and it slowed us some but we were making time and we were going passed the town of Rolla on the north west side. The next town we would come to was Sullivan, Missouri in about four days. As it got toward dusk John stopped his wagons to start our evening meal. I looked ahead and saw a large group of Indians on horseback in front of us. I called for Trent Arthur to get A K.

"He's already with them," Trent said, "He saw them earlier and rode up to talk with them."

A K came back and went to dad and I rode over to see what he had to say. We didn't need any more trouble with Indians, no Cavalry near here to help us.

"Osage tribe boss," A K said, "We are going to go through their territory and they don't want their sacred burial ground torn up by the cattle. They will help us drive the cattle around it at daybreak for the fee of five steers."

"Five steers?" Dad questioned. "You tell them to show us where it is and we will go around it."

"That's just the answer they are expecting Boss," A K told dad, "Osage have been pretty friendly to whites for quite a while now, but this bunch is looking for trouble. Maybe I

can talk them into four steers Boss but we better take what
they give us or we're going to have a fight on our hands."
"OK, talk to them," Dad said, "See what you can do."
A K rode back to the Osage group and they talked for quite
a while waving hands and pointing and speaking in a
threatening manor. Finally A K came back and said they
would be back at daybreak to guide us through.
"Good," Dad said, "How many steers is it costing?"
"Six," A K answered, "And the longer we talked it was
going to cost more. Best take it Boss."
"Six? I thought they wanted five."
"They did Boss, but they said they could be as bull headed
as you and the longer we argued the more they would
want."
I could see dad was really scalding over this but we sure
didn't need anymore trouble. He got off his horse and gave
it to Carlen and went to have a drink of whisky. He was
perturbed. We ate our meal and I rolled a smoke and
Amber and I sat by the fire and had a drink. We talked for a
while and some of the men joined us here and there. Mostly
small talk and some discussion about the Osage Indians
took place. Finally Amber and I rolled out some blankets
and turned in for the night. It was a little cool and it felt
good to snuggle.

Chapter Thirty

In the morning I was awakened by Cookie John banging on a cast iron pot lid letting all know breakfast was ready. Hot coffee, meat gravy and biscuits. It warmed us up and was very good. As we saddled up I noticed the Osage Indians were talking to A K making plans to start the drive. There were about fifty to sixty of them dressed for battle and war paint on their faces. They were a frightening looking bunch but A K said not to worry about it as they were just trying to intimidate us and show their bravery. I hoped that was all and I could see the men were up tight and nervous about it.

Arnie hollered to move the herd and as we moved forward the Osage split up and got on both sides of the cattle at the front and started to string them out and off we went. The mountains here were not like the ones we had in Texas or the Arkansas plains. They were green with trees and foliage. We were in a valley, the trail was tight and we kept the cattle as best we could on the dirt road that wound though it.

The Buff was still in the front of the herd with the lead steers acting like he was one of the bosses. The Osage weren't sure what to make of this oddity but they kept away from him. Traveling in this valley the air was cool as it took time for the sun to top over the mountains but it still didn't get hot by any means. We took a break for lunch and then continued on. In a couple of hours we came to the Osage burial grounds. It was an eerie place with feathers, ribbons and furs hanging from poles stuck in the ground with buffalo, deer and wolf skulls littering the area. I was told by A K the dead are usually buried in a rough rock vault, mostly above the surface of the ground, with a covering of flat stones; the body is wrapped round with a blanket, and many trinkets are buried with the blanket. In the winter time when the ground is frozen, or covered with snow, they sometimes use a hollow tree trunk, into which the body is placed. I saw one such case a body had been shoved in head first. I could see some parts of the blanket, with the bones of the feet, apparently sticking out. The Osage strung out along the burial ground border to keep the cattle from intruding into it. We got the herd by without incident, what a relief.

After passing though the Osage came riding up with A K and met my dad riding with Steve.

"They wish to thank you Boss," A K said, "They are happy you honored their sacred ground. It meant a lot to them and they are only taking four steers, not six."

"Tell them I thank them and wish them the best." Dad answered.

A K told them what dad said and the Warriors pointed at dad raised their hands with a whoop, turned and rode off. I and everyone else were glad that was over and done. The herd moved on through the valley at a quicker pace now that we had no obstacles to worry about. After three days Dad said we were getting close to Sullivan. As I was telling him I would go into town and see if Mom had sent any telegrams Mr. Witt rode up. "Boss, can I and Miss Barbara ride into town and find a preacher so we can tie the knot and get hitched so to speak."

"Richard," Dad answered, "I don't see a problem with that a' tall. In fact, stay the night and catch up in the morn. Brad's going into town; he can be a witness for 'ya."

"Thanks Mr. Charlie, that's great of ya."

"No problem Mr. Witt, you have a nice time. Brad take Amber with you and you can ride back with them. Check to see if Cookie John and the men need anything before you leave." I told him I would check with them and I knew Amber would be real happy to go. I told Amber to get what she needed together for the ride into town.

"Brad it will be so nice to get a hot bath," Amber said with a smile, "and it will be real nice to be alone with you for a time." She galloped her horse to Miss Harris's wagon to get her things. I checked around to see what anyone needed and packed my gear and I rode to Miss Barbara's wagon. Ce Ce was going to handle the wagon on the trail while Richard and Barbara were in town. We got to Sullivan in about forty minutes. It was a small town but well laid out and clean looking. We asked around and they told us there was a hotel of good size, serving meals, with a good reputation just at the end of the street. We rode to the hotel, tied off our horses and walked into the lobby. It was very big hotel for such a small town. And it was very nicely laid out with expensive plush furniture in the lobby, curtains on the windows and a nice hardwood counter to sign customers in. I could see a large dining room in the back set up with tablecloths and settings. An elderly man maybe in his sixties walked up to meet us.

"Howdy folks," He said, "Can I help you? I am Ray Ernes the owner of this establishment. How can I be of service?"

"We need two rooms," Richard told him, "For one night. But first do you know of a preacher man that can perform a marriage? The lady and I want to wed."

"Why yes I do sir. Mr. Keith Young is the preacher in town. A very nice young man. Moved here from Florida a couple years back. He'd be happy to help you and you can do it here if you like. We can serve refreshments for you afterward if you for a small fee."

"That would be just fine," Richard answered, "Is that OK with you Hon."

"That would be very nice Richard," Miss Harris replied, "It will be a fine wedding here."

"OK then," Mr. Ernes said, "Let's get your rooms set for you and you can get a hot bath while I'm getting things set up for you. I'll send for Mr. Young and we will figure on being ready in an hour or so."

 We signed in for our rooms then Richard and I walked the horses to the livery stable and got them taken care of. I then walked to the post office to see if Mom had sent any telegrams. She had sent one saying all was well and not to worry. Rhett Berman has been stopping by with some of the Berman hands quite often to help keep things running smoothly at the ranch. I sent her a reply telling her I would get a message to her when we got to St. Louis. We then returned to the hotel. The rooms were very nice with soft down beds and pillows. They also had tubs with curtains around them and hot water ran from the faucet. As Amber was bathing I looked out the window and a stage pulled up and six people got out and came into the hotel. They even had a man at the hotel to carry in the luggage. We later found out why the hotel was so big and plush. It was the stage and railroad traffic going to St. Louis from Springfield. A lot of high rollers rode these stages. The train depot was destroyed during the war that divided the Nation, but the trains still stopped there.

 After bathing and dressing for the wedding in fresh shirts and denims we met down stairs and Mr. Ernes introduced us to the Reverend Keith Young. He was a very polite young man and did a very nice job with the wedding ceremony. After the ceremony was over Richard kissed

Miss Barbara, she was very happy, it showed in her eyes. He then paid Mr. Young for the ceremony and thanked him. Then Mr. Ernes took us to the dining room where a table was set up with snacks, wine, punch and whiskey. There were several people sitting at tables smiling and waving at the new Bride and Groom.

"Yall come join us," Richard said to them, "This has been a long time a coming.

There be plenty for all you folks. Come join our fun."

Several of the guests came over and congratulated the newly weds and enjoyed the snacks and refreshments. After a lot of hand shaking and hugs we retired to a table for dinner. The special tonight was beef rib roast they were cooking over a grill in the dining room with various vegetable for side entrées. We sat had a few drinks and talked for a while, the meal was perfect. Wanting to get an early start in the morning we said goodnight to each of the guests in the room and retired to our rooms. I looked out the window and another stage had pulled up. This was a busy hotel for such a small town.

Chapter Thirty One

 We woke at dawn and went downstairs for breakfast and
coffee. After paying Mr. Ernes for our accommodations we
walked to the livery stable to get our horses. Richard saw a
buckboard sitting by the stable in very good condition. He
talked to the owner and found it was for sale at a very
reasonable price and it came with the harness. We hooked
up the horse Miss Barbara was riding to the buckboard put
our gear in the back and off we went to find the herd. Mr.
and Mrs. Witt looked very happy riding side by side in
style.
 We caught up to the drive late that afternoon. I told Dad
about Mom's telegram and help from the Berman's, he got
a chuckle out of that. He told me we were about five days
from St. Louis. I'll be glad when this is over and I hope
without any more problems. We stopped for our evening
meal and all the hands came by to congratulate the newly
weds'. After we ate the Mexican Vaqueros brought some
guitars and played and sang for us. John passed out some
jugs for us to have a drink or two. After our little party we
stoked the fire and went to get some rest. Richard and
Barbara went to her wagon and we laughed to ourselves as
Ce Ce took some blankets and got into the new buckboard.
 We awoke in the morning at daybreak and the air was
chilly indeed. I got some coffee for Amber and we waited

for Cookie John to finish breakfast. We had two fires going and almost everyone was huddled around a fire with a blanket wrapped around them trying to warm up.

John had a good meal for us and it felt good to have some hot food in our inners.

Arnie hollered to move 'em out and we started the cattle for St. Louis. We saddled up our horses and they were feeling pretty frisky with this cold air. Some of the horses as long as we have had them still bucked every time we got in the saddle but when the weather was cold it was worse. The buffalo was up in front of the herd acting like he was the boss. Several of the lead steers were with him and a cow. I just can't believe he's stuck with us so long. I guess he just got lonely on the range by himself. The trail wound though the mountain pass littered with rock and debris slowing down the herd a little. It felt good to know we had only four or so days to go baring any trouble. We have had some excitement along this journey but only one stampede. I think most of us feared that more than Indian attacks. A stampede is frighting and can be deadly and a loss of cattle. We lost a few but on our trail we picked up several strays. Our herd now totaled over thirty eight hundred.

The nights were getting a lot cooler and the days were not getting hot at all, maybe in the high sixties to low seventies. Had to wear a light jacket all day as the wind going through the mountains valley made it feel cooler than it really was. I saw several deer and a wolf occasionally, but the wolves didn't bother our cattle. I didn't see any cougars but we heard them at night. That worried us a little. As they could start a stampede if the cattle got their scent. I saw A K ride out and talk to some Indian braves here and there but they were friendly, just curious. One night we had four braves join us for our evening meal and they meant us no harm, they just wanted a good warm meal and coffee. One gave Amber a very nice bead necklace. A K warned us not to give them any whisky or wine as that could cause trouble. Indians couldn't handle alcohol very well.

We were passing just south of Eureka Mo. and Richard Witt asked my Dad if he could run into town to pick up some items for Mrs. Witt and it wouldn't take long at all. Dad said that would be fine but take someone with him just in case. Richard asked around and Matt Barnes said he would go with him.

Eureka was a small town with about one hundred houses, a country store, hotel and a saloon. Richard and Matt tied their horses at the store front and went inside. It only took a few minutes for Mr. Witt to get what he needed and Matt got some fixin's for smokes for himself and some of the men. They paid the store keeper and went outside.

"Want 'a get a shot of whisky, Matt?"

"Sure Richard," Matt answered, "I could use a couple."

They entered the saloon and went to the bar. There weren't many men in there at the time.

"Howdy boys," the bartender said, "What ya' haven?"

"A couple of shots of your good whisky." Matt said and threw a silver dollar on the bar. The bartender put out two glasses and poured some whisky into each.

"Richard Witt," a cowhand hollered, "How the hell are ya?" Richard turned around to see who it was and a smile came to his face.

"Marty Hurr, how you been doing?" Richard answered, "Ain't seen ya in years.   What 'ca do 'in these here parts Marty?"

"Been workin' at the stock yard in St. Louie, how bout you?"

"Head 'in for the stock yard myself, Marty, gotta' deliver a bunch of cattle from Texas in a couple of days."

"That must be the ones Mr. Swift's been expecting, he be glad to get 'em I spec. That's all he's been talk' in bout for days" They shook hands and patted each others back.

"What's that a leather rope?" A cowhand at a table asked as he and a man with walked toward the bar.

"That's a bull whip," Marty replied, "He's a Florida cracker. They use 'em to herd cattle instead of a rope."

"Sounds kind 'a silly." The cowhand said. "What 'ca do with it?"

"Stand back." Richard said and he rolled the whip out and swung it forward and it made a crack like a pistol.

"He's faster with that whip than most with a gun." Marty Hurr told the cowhand.

"I doubt that," The cowboy replied.

"Tell ya what ya' do fellow," Marty said, "empty yer gun and draw it on him if 'in ya want 'a see." The man emptied his revolver and put it back in his holster.

"O K hot shot," He said, "Let's go for it cracker boy." With that Richard rolled out his bullwhip and told him to go for his gun. The man smiled and nodded his head with a grin on his face. They looked at each other for a couple of seconds and the cowhand went for his gun. As he pulled it out, quick as lighting Richard struck with his whip and pulled the pistol from his hand. The cowhand looked confused.

"That was just luck," He said, "let's do it again." Richard nodded his head and the man went for his gun and again Richard pulled from him again. This got he cowhand mad. He loaded his gun put in his holster and told Richard to do it again.

I ain't no fool," Richard said, "You loaded yer gun, I ain't look 'in for no trouble."

"Do it again or I'm gonna' shoot ya either way." The cowboy said and with that his buddy stepped beside him and told Richard, "Ifin' he don't I will." Mat Barnes walked next to Richard and said. "Don't even think about it boys, funs over and I mean it."

The cowhand went for his gun and Richard flipped his whip but when it pulled around the man's hand the gun went off. Richard spun around and he dropped to one knee holding his left arm. The man with him went for his gun and Matt drew his pistol firing two shots so fast it was one long blast and both men fell back shot dead center in the chest. Then Matt looked around the room but no one moved.

"You OK Witt?" Matt asked.

"Got me in the arm Matt, not real bad though, didn't hit the bone."

"Somebody call the Doc." The bartender hollered. "Get Doc John MacKay over here to treat this man. Somebody get the sheriff and get the undertaker too!"

A couple of men ran out of the saloon. The sheriff was the first to come in.

"What's going on here? "He demanded.

"Those two dead cowboys were going to shoot this here tall guy," The bartender said, "and his buddy here drilled them to defend him. They were just playing at first but those two carried it too far."

"That's right sheriff," a man in the saloon said, "It was fair an square, self defense. They was going to shoot this here tall fella' for sure."

"OK then," The sheriff replied, "Help the undertaker get
'em out of here. Looks like your gonna be O K fella'. The
Doc's on the way, sorry you had a bad run in here. I don't
cotton to this happening in our town."
 The sheriff patted Richard on the back and walked out. A
young man in his late thirties came in carrying a black bag.
 "I'm Doctor John MacKay, let's have a look at that
wound. Here sit in this chair." He pulled a chair over for
Richard and got one for himself and started to
look over the wound.
 "Where you from, my friend?" He asked
 "All over," Witt answered, "Started in Florida and recently
from Texas and going to Utah to find land for the wife an
I."
 "Florida's an up and coming state," Doc MacKay said, "I
am going to move there one of these days lots of
opportunity there. You got a clean flesh wound here. No
bone damaged, should heal nicely. I am going to put some
stitches it to close it.
It'll be sore for a while. Keep it clean and bandaged." Doc
MacKay stitched Richards wound and bandaged it. He
patted Richard on the back and told him the city would pay
for his service.
 "I hope the rest of your journey goes well, take care of that
wound. Keep it clean." The Doctor shook his hand and
went outside.

"How about a drink on the house?" The bartender asked Richard. "You too, lightning." Pointing to Matt Barnes. Matt looked at Richard, shook his head in despair thinking he was never going to get away from handling a gun but he knew he would have to wear one to stay alive. He thought to himself, I changed my name and faked my death as Chuck Shoemaker but it doesn't seem to go away. He patted Richard Witt on the back and they stepped to the bar.

"Thanks Matt, "Richard said to him, "He'd a got me if you hadn't been here."

"Glad I was here Richard."

"See ya in St. Louie Marty," Richard told him, "Good to see ya again."

"Good to see you again Richard, I'll tell Mr. Swift you're a coming. I'll ride with you for a while if 'n ya don't mind."

"OK Marty, let's get packing."

Chapter Thirty Two

Richard, Matt and Marty caught up with us in time for our lunch break. Miss Barbara saw Richards bloody shirt and came running to meet him. Richard explained what had happened and told her all would be just fine and not to worry. She hugged him and told him not to over do his arm and let it heal. He smiled and told her again everything is just going to be fine. We ate our lunch and Arnie hollered "RO-L-L-L-L 'EM OUT!" We got in the saddle and started pushing the cattle in an easterly heading just south of St. Louis. Marty Hurr said he was going on. Come evening time we were close to the stock yard and would be there the next day. Finally this drive is coming to an end. I thanked the Lord for watching over us and for not losing a man or have any seriously injured. I will be so glad when this is over and I can get back to Pigeon Forge with Amber.

Cookie John passed out some jugs and prepared our meal, roasted goat. Don't ask me where he got the goat. The meal was good and we all had a swig or two of the whiskey from the jugs. The Mexican Vaqueros gathered around the fire with their guitars and played songs and we all sang along the best we could.

I rolled a smoke and had a cup of coffee before hitting the shelter with Amber. There was a chill in the air so I threw an extra blanket on her and snuggled up.

At the crack of dawn Cookie rang the come an get it bell and everyone rolled out of their wraps. Sausage, gravy and biscuits with coffee was really good choice for a chilly morning. We were just south of town and Marty Hurr rode up and told us he would show us the way to the yard. We saddled up and started to move the herd. I didn't realize just how big St. Louis was. It's the biggest city I've ever seen. It just sprawled out over such a large area. As we got close to the stockyard pens riders came out to help us drive the cattle to the pens. The Buff balked as if he knew it was a dead end and wouldn't go in.

"Just leave him alone," My Dad said, "He'll do what he wants but he's not going anywhere. Keep the lead steers with him and that big brown cow he seems to like so much. He's a little sweet on her" The men all got a laugh from that remark.

A man dressed in a suit came riding up and asked for Charlie Lassiter.

"I'll get 'em fer ya." Don Volsch told him and rode off to get my Dad. Steve and Don came back with Dad and I rode over to meet them where the man in the suit was waiting.

"You must be Mr. Swift!" My Dad said to him.

"That's me for sure and you are Mr. Lassiter?"

"Yes sir I am. Good to meet you."

"It's good to meet you also Mr. Lassiter glad you made it when you did. August is almost gone. Got a lot of work to do Sir, and you made it in time."

"I am glad we did Mr. Swift." Dad replied. "It wasn't a cake walk but we got it done just like you asked."

"You sure did my man. If you can give me a couple of men to work with my men
we will get a head count so to get you paid."

"Brad, Steve you go give Mr. Swift's men a hand." Dad told us.

"You brought some good looking cattle, Mr. Lassiter. I'll pay you top dollar for them. Glad you could get them to me."

Steve and I rode with Mr. Swift to get a head count with his men. The Buffalo was with his lady friend and the few lead steers eating grass out side the stock pens. Mr., Swift asked what we were going to do with the Buff and I told him I didn't know what Dad had planned for him. We got with Mr. Swift's men and started counting. It took us quite a while to finish the count and it came up to thirty eight hundred and thirty three. We then rode back and found my Dad.

"We got the count Mr. Lassiter," Swift said, "And I'm going to pay forty two dollars a head. I'll get your money together and we'll meet at my office."

"Thank you Sir," Dad replied, "Sounds fair enough." They shook hands and Mr. Swift rode off.

"That's one hundred sixty thousand nine hundred eighty eight dollars boys." Dad told us. "We did real well. Let's go get our money."

We rode to Mr. Swift's office and walked inside.

"How about a shot of good Irish whiskey Boys?" Mr. Swift asked. We all said yes and he lined up some glasses for us and poured.

"Here's to your health and safety fellows." We all tipped it down. It had a different flavor than most whiskies I've tried before and was smooth indeed.

"Here's your money in brand new good ole American dollars."

I have never seen that much money at one time. Dad counted it out and gave Steve and me our share.

"That's forty thousand two hundred forty six my boys." Dad said with a big grin on his face. We all shook hands and Mr. Swifts also.

"What are you going to do with the Buffalo?" Swift asked.

"Take 'em back to Texas and let him roam the ranch." Dad replied "He's earned a place there if he will follow us back."

"Good for him." Mr. Swift said, "Hope he has a good long life. Let's have another drink men and I gotta to get to work." We each drank one more and thank Mr. Swift. I carried out my money and put it in my saddle bags. I can't wait to see the look on Amber's face when she see's all that money. We rode back to camp and Dad paid the men from his and Mom's share. Steve and I offered to help with our part but Dad said he wouldn't hear of it.

"You boys keep your money," He said, "You darned sure earned it." Amber declined her pay and told Dad she would share mine. My Dad got a laugh out of that and patted me on the back and told me; "You got a good woman son."

We had a party to celebrate our success and Cookie John made us a great meal with a steer calf. We didn't ask him where he got it as we didn't have any I knew of. We all had some drinks before eating and then got some coffee and sat down to our meal. It was really a good meal and a nice time for us to mingle with the men not worrying about cattle. We all hung around the fire until it got late. After a lot of hand shaking and hugging with the men we retired for the evening. I had no trouble getting to sleep and had the saddle bags by my side for safe keeping. Tomorrow I would have to send a telegram to my Mom and Patti to let them know we were coming back and all was well. Then I would have to make connections for a train back to Tennessee. Dad and the men would be heading out in the morning with the Buff and his lady cow friends for Lufkin Texas. Dad figured it would take less time going home as they could travel faster. I just hoped they wouldn't run into any trouble on the way back.

In the morning Mr. Swift came to camp to bid us goodbye and asked Dad if he would do another drive in the coming spring. Dad told him he would let him know after he talked it over with Mom and the men. Mr. Swift told me he had a telegraph in his office and I could send all I wanted for free. He also told us he was waiting for two more drives to come in. One from Oklahoma and one from Kansas but they were not as large as ours had been. Mr. Swift was quite a man. He walked around and shook every mans hand and tipped his hat to the ladyies before returning to his office.

Richard Witt came over to say goodbye as he and Miss Barbara were going to
head out to Oklahoma and seek their fortune. Josh came over to see Amber.

"Missy Amber, I am going with the Witt's," He told her, "Mr. Richard offered me a job at their new found ranch they are going to settle on. I've been watching over you for many years. You and your Dad always made me feel like I was family and I am proud to have served you. Mr. Brad here will do a fine job of that from now on."

"Yes Josh, you were part of our family," Amber replied, "You're a fine man and I am glad Mr. Witt is taking you on and I know you will do him well."

Amber gave Josh a hug and a kiss. They both had tears in their eyes.

"Bye Missy, I'll miss you"

"Goodbye Josh, I will miss you also and I will name one of my son's after you. God bless and be safe."

It even choked me a little. Josh had been taking care of Amber for years like a sister and he will be a fine addition to the Witt's new undertaking. I walked around and shook hands with all the men. Matt told me he was returning with Dad as he offered him a job at the ranch.

"Thanks for all your help Brad." He told me. "I'm going to try to make a go of it and hope to have a ranch of my own some day."

"Glad I could help you Matt. Chuck is a thing of the past now and Matt moves on." We shook hands and he thanked me again. Steve came to me with a big smile on his face.

"It was good to have you Brad," He said, "Hope to see you again. Love ya brother."

"Love you too Steve," I answered, "Come see us in Pigeon Forge, your welcome any time." We gave each a hug and shook hands. Dad came to me and patted me on the back.

"It was so good to have you son and your young lady," He said, "Hope all goes well for you two and have plenty of young-ins' so Mom Becky can spoil 'em. I want you to keep in touch my boy, and come see us when you can."

"Maybe you can talk Mom into coming to Tennessee Dad. Pretty country there."

"I'll see what I can do," He replied, "But I know when you have the first young-in Miss Becky will wanta' get there to start spoiling it for sure."

"Spoil for sure is right dad, no doubt about it." We hugged and shook hands, he hugged Amber and told her what a great job she did and how happy he was to have her in the family.

"Well Dad we got a train to catch, don't forget to telegram Mom form time to time on your way back to keep her informed. Love ya Dad!" I shook his hand.

"Hope to see you soon son." He patted me on the back and hugged Amber as we turned to get on the buckboard with the man Mr. Swift provided for us to get to the train depot Dad said;

"Hey Son, if-in we get that drive together next spring for Mr. Swift, you want-ta join us?" It stopped me in my tracks and I shook my head and I turned with a smile on my face.

"Dad! That was my Last Drive."

I wish to thank you for your purchase. Be sure to keep your eye out for the printing of the sequel to this book; Texas Bound, coming soon.

Made in the USA
Columbia, SC
22 November 2022